FIC   Gullard, Pamela K.

Breathe at every
other stroke.

$22.00

DATE			

AUG   1996

BAKER & TAYLOR

Breathe

at every other stroke

PAMELA GULLARD

$\mathcal{B}$reathe
at every other stroke

stories

METROPOLITAN BOOKS
Henry Holt and Company
New York

Metropolitan Books
Henry Holt and Company, Inc.
Publishers since 1866
115 West 18th Street
New York, New York 10011

Metropolitan Books™ is an imprint of
Henry Holt and Company, Inc.

LIBRARY OF CONGRESS CATALOGING-IN-PUBLICATION DATA
Gullard, Pamela K.
Breathe at every other stroke: stories / Pamela Gullard.
p.   cm.
1. Manners and customs—Fiction.   I. Title.
PS3557.U446B73   1996   95-49108
813'.54—dc20   CIP

ISBN 0-8050-4385-3

Henry Holt books are available for special promotions and
premiums. For details contact: Director, Special Markets.

First Edition—1996

Designed by Kathryn Parise

Printed in the United States of America
All first editions are printed on acid-free paper. ∞

1   3   5   7   9   10   8   6   4   2

For Mike

Contents

Some Say Fire   1

My Father's Brothers   21

Jump, Jack   31

Only the Lonely Heart   57

The Uncertainty Principle   77

Does Your Tattoo Show?   89

Chinese Tulip   107

You Can See Jupiter with the Naked Eye If
  You Know Where to Look   125

Lifetime Achievement   141

Immortal Buttons   157

Breathe at Every Other Stroke   169

Some Say Fire

I was waiting for them to blow up the Dumbarton Bridge. It was the old drawbridge I had crossed so often when I lived with my mother in San Jose and took singing lessons from my aunt over the San Francisco Bay in Fremont. Now the bridge seemed sad and obsolete. Just north, the new suspension bridge running parallel to it already carried a heavy flow of commuter cars high above the swells.

On the shore, about a mile or so away, I sat on top of a huge Hetch Hetchy water pipe as wide as a man is tall and gazed at the old bridge. My dream of becoming a singer seemed sad, too, and almost obsolete. There was $224 left in my savings account after this last all-out effort to get started as a singer before I hit twenty-five. If something didn't turn up soon, I would have to go back to my accounting job at Compu Corporation. I would spend the rest of my days alone in my cubicle living for the satisfying but tiny ping of balancing the accounts at the end of the month. It occurred to me that a wiser person would have gotten a new dream up and running before the old one was blasted.

The pipe I was sitting on was cradled in scaffolding a few feet off the ground and ran across a strip of marsh to the edge of the bay. My legs, spread out before me, were stiff from the penetrating cold of the metal, and in my back was a sore knot. To my left, a black guy wearing a tam sat eating a tuna fish sandwich. A legal notice at the back of the *Times Tribune* had said the army would dynamite the old bridge at 10:30 A.M. Thursday. It was already 12:23. The delay made me long for yet dread the explosion even more.

How many times had I crossed that bridge? It rested right on the water so that, in a storm, waves came scudding across the center line. I would arrive at my aunt Celia's apartment feeling as if I had practically swum there. Aunt Celia, standing at the piano with one hand on the keys, would throw back her shoulders and exhort me to sing as if I owned the world.

"I don't own the world," I would say, my sheet music in hand.

"Pretend."

"OK. Maybe it's possible while I sing, but what about when I stop?"

"On stage, the time between songs is almost as important as the music. Your beautiful voice won't get you anywhere without presence."

"How about if I just try for California?"

I shut my eyes not so much to rest as to ignore the guy eating his sandwich. While you're singing, the audience loves you and you can feel it. They close their eyes when you do. Their clapping at the end of the song washes over you like a thousand hands touching you.

The audition at the Skylit Basement the day before had gone pretty well at first. I sang a complete set before the manager stopped me. Hal Patterson has a shiny forehead and a cowlick, which he tugs at as he speaks. "Got any patter?" he asked.

"I don't talk," I said. "I just sing."

He seemed to accept that and my hopes rose, but then he had called that morning to say that my singing was lyrical but he needed more, uh, personality. So sorry.

The guy in the tam finished his sandwich, wiped his hands on his jeans, and reached into an inner pocket of his pea jacket. He took out binoculars with a broken strap and looked across the water. "Nothing happening," he said. I hadn't been sure he could talk. "You think they gave us a bum steer?" He tapped his stubbled chin meditatively, as if pondering the mysteries of other people's plans. He himself didn't look like he'd kept a very strict schedule of late.

"I hope not," I said with a fervor that surprised even me. "I mean, I want to see a huge, fiery, *loud* explosion that rocks our hearts." It occurred to me that audiences are looking for hope even more than for music. Maybe they want to watch the singer unfold herself, see her reach for them and grab hold.

The bridge in the midday sun had become a shiny line across the bay. My early life had been laid out on that span. In high school, I drove back and forth twice a week for my singing lessons, and it was on the long, monotonous stretch of the Dumbarton that I thought about my first, quiet boyfriends and how different they were from the loud men who took out my mother and my aunt. I made up songs as I drove, and I devised big plans for my future. All my past seemed laced onto the bridge, waiting now to be blown up.

At two o'clock I got up quietly. My legs were stiff and unsteady. The black guy's head was sunk so low in his high blue collar that I couldn't tell if he was asleep or not. I blew him a kiss and trotted over the gravel and weeds to my Volvo, which was salmon pink from years of oxidation.

Later that evening, I lay on my bed listening to my tape of *Sticky Fingers* play over and over. Finally reaching over to click it off, I dozed.

At three o'clock in the morning I awoke. The room had cooled and was as dark as the deep, rich center of a perfect black note.

By feel, I put on a flannel shirt for bed and got under the quilt. It was my aunt Celia who first took up with the Tacky Brothers, as I called them. She moved in with the one who sold vacuum cleaners, and then my mother started seeing his brother. When I was seventeen, my mother suddenly went on vacation with the one who said he owned a ranch in Texas. She left a note telling me to spend the week at Celia's. I drove across the Dumbarton to my aunt's new place in the hills, but neither she nor her Tacky Brother was there. Celia said later that they had gone to an Elvis sound-alike contest in L.A. and decided to stay a few nights. It was never clear whether she had forgotten I was coming or had just not been told. In a wink, I was alone. I drove back to my mother's apartment.

Finally, on Sunday, my mother came into the kitchen with a suitcase in hand. She smelled of alcohol and looked surprised to see me. When she heard about Celia, she shrugged. "You can take care of yourself for a week, I guess."

"Doesn't it matter to you what happens to me?"

"It matters." She swayed. The brother came in the door and put his thick arms around her waist. "But obviously you're all right," she said.

"I'm not all right," I shouted. Those were my last words to my mother for a year. At first, my mind was blank and I couldn't name my emotions. Then I realized I felt expendable. Speech was pointless. Nothing I said would keep my mother from her next Tacky adventure. My silence deepened. At school I hardly spoke. The final months of my senior year I cut chorus a few times, then gave up my music altogether. It was an act of spite, but of course it hurt only me. I took the clerical job at Compu Corporation and didn't tell anyone when I got an apartment. I just moved out.

Next morning, the same guy was sitting in the same spot wearing his pea jacket and the tam. I wasn't even sure he had moved. "Hi," I said.

We exchanged names. He said he was called Roy, as in the French for *king*. He gave an amused snort. He took out the binoculars and looked at the distant span, though we both knew this was more a matter of form than any real expectation of new developments. He put the binoculars down on his thigh. "After the explosion, they'll turn the stub ends into fishing piers," he said.

"Oh?" A sea tern circled us. "Do you fish?"

"Not anymore." He wound the strap around the binoculars. "The last fish I caught was when I helped some guys with a sturgeon on the Rogue River, border of Oregon. The sturgeon lays at the bottom, see, and waits. You raise him with grappling hooks. That fish was three hundred pounds. Took us two hours."

"Did you work on a boat for a living?"

He snorted as if that were funny too. The deep creases from his broad nose to his chin spread as he smiled. "Not for a living," he said, with an inflection that mocked my politeness.

"Do you have a family?" I figured sitting on a pipe together for two mornings entitled me to some questions.

A short sigh. A moving of the binoculars from one thigh to another. He looked at me. This day was sunny but no warmer than the previous one. His black-gray hair shone beneath the hat, whether from oil he'd put on that morning or from sweat, I couldn't tell.

He raised his eyebrows. "Can you keep a secret?"

I hadn't been expecting secrets, though I sensed he was an outsider. Was he a spy? Did he murder someone? He didn't seem violent. But I shrugged. I didn't plan to be bound by his secrets.

He spoke anyway. His tone was low but clear, each word pronounced separately and distinctly. "I like men," he said.

His meaning was just dawning on me when he continued, his voice slightly higher and faster. "In my day, someone like me didn't get much of a chance. Double trouble. My own brother caught me with a friend of his and tried to drown me with a garden hose. He turned it on flat out and held my nose. He crammed the hose to the back of my throat while he called me names I won't repeat to you. The water ripped into my lungs, into my sinuses." He sighed, shifted position. "So mostly I lay low. There were a couple of years when I thought I'd shake my low-profile habit, but with AIDS most everyone either has someone already or is waiting things out."

I was stunned by his story. I thought of his brother, my mother. Did the most important people always turn away in the end? Moments passed. I realized Roy was watching my face for a response. He didn't seem the kind who trusted his tale to just anyone. It must have come out because we were the only two people sitting on a pipe with miles of marsh and bay stretching away from us. What could I say?

"Did you drown?" I asked.

He smiled. He adjusted his hat so that it barely skimmed his left eyebrow. "Yeah," he said. "Went to heaven and guess what I came back as—since I was so good at it?"

I looked at him uncertainly.

He pointed at himself and whooped. "The same—exactly the same."

We laughed and let it die, and then laughed some more. Then he sobered. His face was wet. "So my job is a little of this, a little of that." He turned his eyes back to me. "What's yours?"

At first I didn't have an answer, then I smiled as I thought about the singing. "My job is just to be adored," I said. "Right now I'm unemployed."

He chuckled. "Actually that's my job too."

We waited. We waited some more. A few people came, faced the bridge for a while, and left, shaking their heads. The bridge was an act that never came on. I felt restless, like an audience that has bought tickets in good faith and is about to turn ugly. Roy was deep in his prelunch nap.

The hot noon sun warmed the pipe. My mother and aunt were both in Texas now. I couldn't tell which brother they were living with. They sent me postcards, as if they were permanently on vacation, which is different from being unemployed.

I tried to think of patter. Hi! I'm Candace Dillinger and I'm going to sing for you an old Scottish ballad called "The Raggle-Taggle Gypsies, O!" The first version of this song was called "Johnny Faa" after the Johnny Faa who was hanged in 1624 for disobeying the government decree banishing gypsies from Scotland.

No, too historical. Too gloomy. The audience is out for a good time. Not hangings.

Hi! I'm Candace Dillinger and I'm going to sing a Billie Holiday song for you, "What a Little Moonlight Can Do." This is a song from the depression about love and happiness, kisses and heaven.

Who do I think I'm kidding? Schmaltz, even good schmaltz, isn't exactly what they want these days. Need something more updated, more punchy, more now.

Hi! I'm Helen Reddy and I'm going to sing for you "I Am Woman." (Pause.) Stand back.

I wished I had my harmonica to help me think. I bought it the day I quit my job, the day I started singing again. Hal said not to use the harmonica at the club. Too sixties. Looks funny in front of a pretty girl's face.

Hi! I'm Candace Dillinger and I'm going to sing "Cockles and Mussels." This is an old Irish folk ballad about a girl who sells seafood. It isn't funny. It isn't upbeat. It isn't twentieth century. I just like the tune.

Blah. Everyone falls asleep.

Roy opened his eyes. He took out his sandwich. I took out mine. (I had made it that morning.) He smiled. I smiled. He loaned me the binoculars for a look.

By three I couldn't stand it any longer. I told Roy I had an errand and I'd be back. He said there was no need—even the army wouldn't blow up a bridge at rush hour. His indifference to whether I returned or not hit me hard. I had thought we were friends.

"I'll be back," I said. "You never know what the armed forces will do." I planned to check my answering machine, get a paper, buy a candy bar, and return quickly to our vigil.

He shrugged.

Was there some small pleasure in my loyalty? I couldn't tell.

In Palo Alto, I called home out of vague hope, not really expecting anything. Hal's voice was on my machine. The regular singer at the club (he and his guitarist called themselves Danny and the Night Dog) had a sore throat. Could I fill in that night?

I put the receiver in its small silver cradle, and the tone device back in my purse. The top of my head was stretching upward, pulling my ears into an alert position. I could hear every tiny rustle of the people walking outside and the whispers of the bay breezes skulking about town. I opened the phone booth and listened to the peeps and scrapes, grunts and murmurs of my world.

I forgot about the newspaper, I forgot about the candy bar, I forgot about Roy and the explosion. I drove home wildly. I threw all my clothes on the bed and tried to put together the sexiest, most lyrical outfit in the world.

In the dark of the nightclub, I stood in front of the audience in a shimmering dress with tiers of sequins at the hips. My moussed hair looked like it had been swept back by a fierce wind. I wore shiny sandals with narrow straps. Very eighties, very punchy.

The big middle-aged man at the table to my left was telling a joke about a porpoise to a young woman who dipped her long fingers into a glass and dragged miniature ice cubes out to suck on. Five women in their forties sat at two round tables pushed together. Their heads were turned toward me but their eyes darted all over the room. It was possible that no one except me knew I was there.

Perching on the very tall stool in the middle of the stage, I tapped the microphone. The sound, so alive and startling to me, didn't faze the audience. My guitar felt slippery, its cord snaking across my foot. Sooner or later I was going to have to say something.

"Hi," I said. "I'm Candace Dillinger and I'm not Danny and the Night Dog. As perhaps you can see."

No laughter. Not even a smile. I turned cold inside. Various joints in my body lost their connection with one another and I expected my fingers to fall off, my kneecaps to roll into the aisle, my ears to plop onto the dusty pink floor.

"Actually," I said, lowering my voice, which had been reaching supersonic levels. "I'm Cyndi Lauper and I just wanna have fun."

The noise hardly abated. The bored young woman continued sucking. The five older ones continued looking and murmuring among themselves. A boy with slick short hair and a girl in a long sweater stood at the bar and vibrated to each other.

"That was a joke," I said, smiling madly at them all.

"Are you going to keep this up all night?" asked the big man. He wore a shirt so thin I could see his nipples.

I sang. My voice wobbled at first, then grew stronger for a couple of songs. No one seemed to notice. I tried to smooth them on out with some B. B. King. The big man rolled his eyes. I attempted to warm him up with the sweet melodrama of the Everly Brothers' "Take a Message to Mary." During the song he discussed Scotch loudly with the waitress—which brand was available and which one was the best.

Halfway into the set, I rested my guitar across my lap. I looked out from the spotlight to the dimness of the audience. "I want to sing for you Janis Joplin's little masterpiece 'Mercedes-Benz,' but I have to tell you that the most important part of the song comes when it's over, when Janis Joplin giggles." I was so confused I could have said anything. "I mean, it's that giggle that flips the song over and makes it even funnier—or rather, sadder—what I mean is that Janis Joplin didn't want a Mercedes exactly. She wanted . . ."

Someone turned up the stage light so I sat in a glow. Why was I trying to explain what Janis Joplin wanted? "She wanted . . ." A few in the audience leaned forward, including the big man. "Something." I dropped my head in embarrassment. They were being entertained by an idiot.

The room became quieter. They were waiting for me. I smiled—what else?—and tried again. "But I can't do the giggle, I mean here, Janis Joplin's giggle—you know, throaty, wise, happy for a moment no matter what." My voice died, came back. "So some of you could do the giggle. I mean, if you've ever wanted something beyond a Mercedes." I stopped there. Certainly I'd said enough.

Janis knew when to quit talking and sing. "Oh Lord, won't you buy me / A Mercedes-Benz?" I loved that song. "My friends all drive Porsches / I must make amends."

The end came all too soon. I braced myself for the sneering titters. But no, almost silence. Then the big man's girlfriend straightened up and gave out a breathy chuckle. There was that slight self-mocking, and the delight. I giggled too— the first time in front of an audience. Even the big man laughed, and then he kissed his girlfriend on the forehead and they leaned into each other.

It was that small bit of hope that got me. I would have done anything to keep their attention and grabbed for the one thing I hadn't tried before. "And next, I'm going to sing you a song I wrote myself, a long time ago, when I was young."

"Last week?" asked the big man, but he was good-natured about it, and everyone laughed. They were listening.

"I wrote it when I was driving across the old Dumbarton Bridge, the one that's being replaced."

They nodded. They lived in Fremont, or in the East Bay hills because it was cheap, and they commuted. For a second, we were commuters together.

"They're going to dynamite the old one, maybe tonight. In fact, it may be blowing up right now."

They looked shocked. I took a breath, the first easy one that night. "This song is about love, which is all I'm really interested in, deep down." They looked dreamy.

They kept that dreamy look during the song. I, too, felt entranced.

But when I came back from my break, the feeling was gone. By the next song, all the joking, gnawing, flirting, sucking, glasses tinkling, and chairs scraping rose even higher than before and I wondered if anyone could hear me.

At 11:30 I scraped myself up and collapsed backstage in the swaybacked overstuffed chair that took up most of the space in the closet Hal called a dressing room.

He leaned against the wall. "Can you come tomorrow if Danny is still sick?"

I uncurled myself and went to the small sink to pour a glass of water, which I gulped down. "Why would you want me?" I asked. "Most of the time they weren't listening."

Hal's face was white and haggard from the long night. He put one foot back against the tan wall. "The audience wants you to be bigger and more beautiful, more thrilling than you actually are. Maybe you haven't learned that yet, but I think you have a chance. A small chance." He smiled.

Angrily I said, "Why does everyone take it upon himself to tell me I need to be more this, more that?"

Hal's voice remained the same. "I didn't say that. I just said you have to make the audience believe that you're more than you are."

I filled the glass again and crumpled into the big chair. "And how do I do that?"

"By being yourself to the nth degree. Like Jack Nicholson. He seems much sexier and more handsome than he really is because he's so much Jack Nicholson."

Hal's kindliness surprised me. "Oh, sure," I said sardon-ically, wishing I could come up with something to match his decency, but I couldn't even manage a smile yet.

Hal went on. "The audience wants you to blast them out of their little selves. Who knows, they might learn something from you. Even you. It's your patter that's got it, like that shy bluesy bit you did after the Janis Joplin, about the bridge. For a minute there, you had them."

"They were just intrigued that a person could dig herself into such a deep hole so fast."

He shook his head. "Not just that." Then a shift of his other foot against the wall. "I know my audiences."

This was his dismissal. He leaned over and patted me on the shoulder. "If Danny's still out, you can try again tomor-row night," he said. "I'll call you." I was grateful he didn't try to cover up the fact that mainly he needed someone to fill the gap.

That night I dreamed of standing in the middle of the bridge, a robed chorus behind me, my mouth wide open but no sound coming forth.

At 5:45 in the morning I rushed into the kitchen and slathered tuna fish on several pieces of bread. My harmonica was on the kitchen counter. I picked it up, cupped my hands around it, then placed it back on the counter.

I threw the sandwiches in a bag and raced to my car. What if the bridge had gone without me? What if Roy had been waiting for me all this time?

The bridge was still there. Roy wasn't sitting on the pipe. Even the sea terns were gone. I sat and shivered, hoping he'd come even more than I hoped for the explosion.

The sun rose and became very hot and I felt plastic, as if, having melted in front of the audience the night before, I could more easily go again. I clung to the pipe. I didn't eat my sandwiches. I didn't check my machine to find out whether Hal needed me again.

In the afternoon I lay lengthwise on the still-cold pipe and waited. The night was cool, then cold. My sweater gave only thin protection against it. I wondered what Roy was doing. I wondered if Danny and the Night Dog were singing or if the stage was empty. I wondered if the bridge would blow and blast me right off the pipe.

The moon came up. A few lights across the bay winked on. I realized that Hal had told me the same thing my aunt had always said—that a soloist needed presence. Probably more presence than I would ever have. I just wasn't the kind to hold an audience the way you must when you're up there alone on the stage. The thought made me very sleepy and I laid my head on my arm.

In my dream Jack Nicholson was on the bridge trying to sing and I was speaking to him the way Hal had spoken to me. "No, no," I said to Jack. "This is all wrong. You shouldn't sing. It's just not Jack Nicholson. You're supposed to talk in that wry, mocking voice you use. That's your job." I snatched the sheet music from his hand and threw it in the water below.

Morning came cold and damp. I thought of my dream and smiled. I had an empty feeling, as of something finished. The tule fog hovered over the water and made the distant bridge look ghostly. I ate a sandwich. The mayonnaise had soaked through the bread. My hair hung in damp strips around my face. No matter. I would wait here at the bottom until that damned bridge blew.

I must have dozed again. I heard a sound at the scaffolding. Was it? Yes, it was Roy climbing onto the pipe. He reached for the scaffolding to pull himself up. His knuckles were grayish, as if dusted with a fine powder. The pocket of his pea jacket caught on a bolt and he delicately released it, then straightened up.

I threw my arms around him. "I'm glad you're here!" I cried.

He rocked back and for a moment I thought he might teeter right off the pipe. I caught his hand, then released it.

He looked at me. "You stoned?"

That hurt. For some reason I had thought he would understand everything. "No, I'm not stoned," I said irritably.

"You look bad."

"And good morning to you!" I brushed my face to be sure there were no crumbs on it.

He shrugged. He sat down in his place. "I thought you were coming back Friday."

Aha, even the sphinx had feelings.

"I had business," I said. I sat beside him in my place.

He chuckled. "Didn't turn out great."

I smiled.

He told me the bridge was scheduled to go at noon. I gave him a wry look. He shrugged again. "What happens happens," he said.

At 10:30 they started coming—young couples with small children in canvas seats on their backs, grandmothers, teenagers, old men. They said there had been a full-page story in Saturday's *Times Tribune* and they wanted to see the bridge blow up. They brought long-nozzled cameras with tripods and six-packs of Budweiser, coolers, binoculars, chairs, and extra jackets. They sat in rows on the gravel path and behind the pipe. They pointed at the bridge and asked one another questions about who would blow it up and where the sticks of dynamite would go.

Noon came and went.

Rumors floated through the crowd. The bridge would go at 12:45. The army was waiting for the tide to rise. To fall. The bridge would go at 1:50.

A tall man of about forty climbed the scaffolding. He wore the double-breasted jacket of a chef's uniform with his jeans. He stood on the pipe, to my right. Several teenagers climbed after him. A man with a pink sweater over his shoulders strode up the path with a long-legged dog at his heels.

Sitting on the pipe, about five feet from Roy and me, was a girl with thick blond hair to her shoulders. She claimed she saw a frogman dive from the bridge. "You can't see that far," said the chef pleasantly. He had a long face, high forehead.

"I can," she said. "I have perfect vision." She and her red-headed girlfriend giggled together. The chef laughed too. He called down to the man with the pink sweater, asking what kind of dog it was.

"A Chesapeake Bay retriever," said the man rather primly, tossing a stick in the water.

The dog romped after the stick and bounded into the water. "Looks like he's a San Francisco Bay retriever," said the chef to Roy. Roy laughed and looked up at the chef.

Helicopters flew overhead. State policemen sped back and forth over the new bridge. This was it. Something was going to happen today.

Many people got tired of waiting and left. We diehards stayed. The blond, who was called Pauline, spotted a puff of dark smoke rising from the raised center of the bridge. We watched with our breaths held back. The black smoke billowed up for ten minutes and then started to dwindle. It turned white.

"They've elected a pope!" said Roy, and the chef gave an appreciative snort. He and Roy had a similar sense of humor.

We took bets on when it would go. I shared my sand-wiches. Roy gave everyone a turn with his binoculars.

Two squad cars parked at the entrance to the new bridge and stopped traffic. The bantering among us slowed. Pauline said she saw a man near the Dumbarton holding a glowing punk. It was 2:53. We became silent. The last car inched up over the arch of the new span and we all watched it drive away.

Then the bridge blew. There was no sound at first. A row of huge smoke columns puffed out along the inverted U and for three seconds we watched in utter silence, transfixed. The black pillars grew even larger and pieces of metal rose in slow motion through the air.

Out of this mesmerizing silence came the sound, a heart-stopping boom that hit Roy so hard a surprised "Oh!" came from his mouth and he grabbed for my hand to steady him-self. We sat still as the explosion washed over us. Then it was gone.

Roy jumped up, whooped, and threw his tam in the air. It sailed up and arced out over the water and we watched it alight delicately. He whooped again and threw his arms around the yahooing chef. Pauline danced up and down the broad back of the pipe. The crowd cheered. The dog re-trieved the tam.

I turned to Roy, whose face shone. "It sounded like the end of the world!" I shouted.

"It did," said Roy.

I clapped his arm, joy rising. I gave him my best deadpan. "We're in heaven!" Laughing people surrounded us.

Roy gave me a nice sardonic look and then surveyed the shore. The long puff of smoke still hovered over the water where the bridge had been. "Looks different from when I was here last." He glanced at the chef and the chef smiled.

I giggled. "I gave you that one."

A crinkling of the eyes. "That you did."

Random cheers for the bridge continued to erupt for a while, then finally died down. Pauline said she had to go home, and the people below us packed their cooler. The man wiped his dog's legs with a towel and the dog and he trotted off together. Roy gave me a nod and left with the chef. Half an hour later, I was sitting alone on the pipe listening to the gentle lap of the waves. A tern squawked overhead.

The soft late-afternoon air wafted across my face. Finally, I climbed off the pipe. I walked slowly across the gravel. I had time. I would go home and take a long shower. I would scat around on some of my own blues pieces. I had been writing them before I lost confidence and switched to covering other people's songs. Then I would pick up the phone and give Danny a get-well call. I would ask him if he wanted to join forces with a singer who could back up almost any of the standards and would like a chance to come forth once in a while with some sweet new tunes of her own.

My Father's Brothers

I thought of the uncles as a single entity. It wore a canary-yellow polo shirt and had several long, sinewy arms. One reached for a bourbon glass—the ice clinking—while another rested on a knee that got sharper from one reunion to the next. Other arms wrapped themselves around me and drew me close so that I could smell the old-man smell and see the tufts of hairs that sprouted from the ears.

The uncles, magically separated into individual men—all plowed—were singing, the aunts at their sides. The aunts had the good voices and remembered the words, but it was the uncles who started the songs.

We were at my father's house in Seattle at the family reunion that took place every other year in some part of the country. I sat next to Uncle Cy, a civil engineer who lived in Des Moines. Periodically I went into the yellow kitchen, which was clean but shabbier than I remembered, and hand-carried an ice cube back to keep the level in his glass high.

"So, Homer," said Cy to my father after the last languid note of "Bye Bye Blackbird" died and before the others figured out the chorus to "Just One of Those Things." "You've learned to cook now."

The murmuring stopped except for one uncle, John, who was a little deaf and was practicing thirds, his eyes rolled to the ceiling, a flop of gray hair puffing out over his forehead every time he tried for a note below his range.

Eight pairs of eyes turned toward my father from all quarters like tiny blinking lights set at intervals. Veined hands recrumpled used napkins at the table, and Uncle Walker, his fingertips yellow with nicotine, restlessly brushed his knuckles together.

This was the closest anyone had come in two days to mentioning my father's divorce.

My father looked at a spot just below the brass chandelier with the electric candles. He said nothing. The lines of his forehead seemed to deepen. His skin glistened. Someone coughed in embarrassment. I willed him to say something, but he was quiet, as he had always been.

The silence was broken by Uncle John, hitting a deep note hitherto unplumbed. "Oh," he muttered, his cheeks pink, his eyes wide. Someone laughed, an aunt giggled, and then the rest of them roared. The singing started again, but I didn't join in. For a moment I disliked my uncles the way I did when I was younger and had not learned that all of us have weaknesses.

Uncle Cy, the oldest, would be the one tacitly appointed to bring up delicate matters. My father's life needed investigation, after all. First his wife had run off—and not even for another man. As if that wasn't enough, Homer had organized the reunion himself. He was the one who had typed the invitation, photocopied it, and mailed it to the four families across the country, just like the aunts did. He had ordered the ham from Hickory Farms for the first night's feast and even had apple pies that looked suspiciously home-baked. No one dared ask him where he'd gotten them. Initially there was some hopeful speculation I'd brought them with me from Oregon, then disappointment when I shook my head no. The uncles chewed their food slowly, crossed their legs uneasily, and looked at my father with worried eyes.

Then there was the question of the shrink. Late the previous night, when everyone was fuzzy and Cy was sprawled on the brown corduroy couch in the living room while Walter leaned awkwardly against the piano, one of the aunts whispered to another that Homer was seeing a *psychiatrist*. The blinking lights snapped toward me and I pretended to be nodding off in my chair, but the matter didn't drop and I heard it again as I stumbled off to bed. I had thought of the uncles as merely quaint, but now I began to sense a buried ferocity in their mutterings. Feeling edgy, I wondered how deeply my father's implacable shift toward new ways provoked them.

Now, a day later, I was still tired. At dusk, I'd driven my father's Buick downtown to the Pike Place Market with his blank check for seven pounds of salmon. When I returned, the uncles were standing around the domed barbecue in the light drizzle giving my father advice on how much charcoal to use and when to light it. As I passed Uncle Cy I saw him nudge Uncle John and mutter that all was lost anyway—a good glow should have been started hours ago. A few minutes later, my father emerged from the kitchen carrying the fish in foil. He placed it on the grill, and the aroma of butter and garlic elicited an "ahh" from the uncles. After a minute, Uncle John nudged Cy back and whispered that the foil would taint the taste. Cy, who relished his role as chief critic and was seldom bothered by inconsistency, responded with a sad nod that Homer was cooking the best he could.

The singing would continue for hours. I wanted to stay up to listen. I loved the old songs and the way they merged into one another as an uncle would start his long-awaited choice on the heels of the last tune's final chorus. But my eyes were heavy.

I brought Cy two ice cubes to hold him for a while and came to my father to say good night. He was caught off guard and he looked bewildered and very tired. He brightened quickly, though, and took my hand. "Thanks for helping," he said, and I kissed him on the forehead.

"It's all right. I want to." He squeezed my hand. For a second we didn't speak, and I felt the easy alliance we'd had when I was very young. But then the aunt leading the way through the many verses of "Wayward Wind" finally ground to a halt, and I realized the uncles were waiting for my father before they started a new song.

The strains of "Down in the Valley" followed me upstairs, became fainter and then louder again as I stood before the heating grate in the bathroom, the duct a perfect musical conduit. I washed my face to "Swing Low Sweet Chariot," and got into my nightie to "My Lord, What a Morning" (the songs were remembered in streaks). I brushed my teeth to the slow, sweet melody of "You'll Never Walk Alone," which I continued to hear as I walked to the end of the hall, where I called my fiancé and told him I was going to stay the full four days of the reunion.

My suitcase lay open as I'd left it in my mother's sewing room, a name that was an old joke. My mother wasn't the kind to sew; instead she spent hours in her sanctuary writing fiery one-act plays and reading for her German literature courses at the University of Washington. The narrow walls and even the ceiling were covered in midnight-blue wallpaper. My mother said she thought better in the dark. Some of her books were still stacked in piles on the floor, and I knew my father had not been in this room since the divorce except to set up the green cot for my visit.

Now I sat on the cot and listened for the music. None. Either there was a lull as someone tried to think of the words or it was the time for drowsy small talk before bed. I hoped I could get to sleep before they came up the stairs and I heard from the bathroom the sounds of old men, one by one, preparing themselves for bed.

But I couldn't fall asleep. Exhausted, I lay awake in the sewing room. Through the separation, my mother, who had always been excitable, had managed to remain the same—a little odd, but in the way she had always been. My father was the one trying new things.

I lay back with the thin pillow propped against the wall and heard the heavy footsteps of the uncles, accompanied by the lighter, quicker sounds of the aunts. I squeezed my eyes shut and pulled the blankets up over my shoulders.

The footfalls went up and down the corridor as each couple found the right room, and the hall light went off, then on, a crack of yellow at my door, as someone creeped back downstairs to get a forgotten item. One uncle took a shower and I heard an aunt laugh.

Then there was quiet and I dozed, my head still propped up against the wall.

The light knock at my door brought me fully awake in a moment. "Yes," I said.

"It's your father. Is it all right if I come in?"

"Yes. Fine." Although I had been home for two days, we had hardly had a chance to talk, and I was glad to be able to assess him without his brothers around. I reached down and picked my sweatshirt off the floor and pulled it on over my nightgown so that he would feel comfortable. "Please, come in." I snapped on the bedside lamp with the crooked flexible head.

"May I sit down?"

"Of course."

He carefully removed a pile of books from my mother's desk chair and brought the chair over to the cot. His hair had gotten a little long behind the ears and it gave him a bedraggled look. I wondered if this was a new style or neglect and couldn't decide which I hoped for. He had the thinness of his brothers, and hollows were beginning to form below his collarbone. They were the kind of men who shrank with age.

"Honey," he said, taking my hand. "I'm scared. I don't think I can go on with this."

"You're doing very well. You're doing fine."

"I'm still doing it for her. I'm still hoping."

"I know," I said. I was always kind to him, whether I felt it or not. He's one of those who need kindness. "But that's all right for now," I said. "You'll find your own way."

"Will I?"

I wanted to pat his head, give him strength.

Uncle Cy seemed to crash through the door, throwing splinters into the air. Actually, the door was open and he just walked in.

He was drunk. "I thought I heard voices. A tête-à-tête in the middle of the night. Homer, I knew you'd turn to family at some stage. Left high and dry. Abandoned!" He raised his hands dramatically. "Up a creek without a paddle. Good God." He began to cry. Then stopped. "But why didn't you come to your big brother first? Wise old Cy. Here, I'll join you." He sat on the floor, his feet sticking out of rayon pajama bottoms. Blue veins bulged along his dry, white ankles.

"Cy, we don't want to be interrupted just now," I said, my voice tight with exhaustion and fear.

Ignoring me, he pointed a finger at my father. "Homer, you need some advice, you know. Take it from Cy—what you want right now is a girlfriend. I know. I've been there. A couple of years ago Joanie got some ideas and I was alone for too long. She had to understand that a man needs a woman. Simple as that."

"Cy," I said. My voice broke. I looked at my father. He sat with his head down, concentrating on his hands. "Cy," I said, "stop it. You're drunk and you're telling us things we don't want to know." My father sat impassive, hoping Cy would go away. My mother had told me it was my father's uselessness that finally drove her from home.

"Listen, Homer," my uncle continued, getting to his knees and leaning toward my father. "A good roll in the hay will fix you right up."

"Cy, please," I said.

My father cleared his throat. He let go of my hand. He grew pale. The cords of his old neck stood out. Silently I urged him on. He wilted, then looked at me, swallowed, and scratched his ear. "Cy," he said.

He smiled as his shoulders relaxed. "My psychiatrist—" He paused, savoring the moment. Cy swayed back. "My psychiatrist tells me I don't have to like the people I love." He paused again, rubbing his forehead. He shifted, leaned forward. Then he shook his head and spoke conspiratorially, brother to brother. "Do you have any idea what that means?"

Cy looked at him, blinked, looked at me, thought for a moment. If he said yes, he would be supporting my father's vague criticism; a no would show ignorance. He opened his mouth, shut it. He stood up, started to say something again, then, with a small nod of his head, turned and left.

My father looked at me and smiled. He leaned back in the chair. "I thought I'd forgotten how to do that," he said.

Jump, Jack

*L*ate at night, Jack, a deliveryman for Floral Magic, jogged along San Francisquito Creek. Sometimes he felt as if he were being chased, at other times as though he were trying to keep up with a fast-moving object. He breathed cool California air and knew that only a fine membrane separated him from his old self, the whacked-out ghost who slept in the dry creek bed with the other drunks, schizos, and dropouts who were too exhausted to catch the Redwood City bus to Human Services. Cops shone their flashlights down the creek every few hours, and the sleeping bodies would jerk awake and swear or scream. Sometimes the men would fight, or the bearded guy who got messages from God through license plates would set fire to the weeds around his rock.

Jack ran the snaking length of San Francisquito Drive. Though he'd left the creek three years ago, he still felt a shiver of surprise when the regular people of Palo Alto waved at him as they walked their dogs. He tried to see himself the way they did—a tall man in his forties wearing Lycra tights and the Stanford sweatshirt he'd bought at Long's Drugs, someone much like them, maybe even a little better since he was exercising nightly, taking care of himself, staying young.

Running faster, he crossed the trestle, stepping carefully. A few years ago, a drunk had stumbled on the tracks and a train had sliced off his head. Jack had known him slightly.

He dashed through the streets of East Menlo. His chest pounded, sweat slid down his neck. Back over the creek at the bike bridge, then past the night-dead stores of Palo Alto to the entrance of his apartment over the Quik Bagel. He had left the downstairs door unlocked to remind himself that he lived in a place where unguarded things were left alone.

He closed the door, shutting out the moonlight, and climbed the steps feeling nicely blown out. With the run under his belt, he could stay ahead of the dreamlike state he'd sunk into down by the creek. For a moment the idea of arriving at a particular place at a particular time—a job, for example—had seemed like nothing more than a skitter bug on the great stream of time.

A man was standing on the upstairs landing. Jack froze, crept backward in the shadows. He knew that people who appeared out of nowhere were usually trouble.

The voice above him said, "It's me. Greg."

His son, a person he hadn't even known existed until Greg had found him in the phone book two years ago. Now Greg called every so often to "shoot the breeze." He was twenty-five and he'd forgiven Jack for disappearing, he said, but Jack hadn't figured out how to act forgiven. His legs got heavy as he climbed the last steps.

"Pop," Greg said, "I knew I'd catch you coming in. I have to tell you—I'm in love." He grabbed Jack's hand in both of his.

He was even taller than Jack and wore a soft suit with big shoulders that made Jack feel shabby. "Please don't call me Pop," Jack said. "It sounds like I've been shot out of something." He unlocked his apartment. Ferris, his big orange cat, jumped off the futon and he scooped her up.

Greg stayed in the doorway. He rarely came in—Jack thought he'd make a good gangster lookout. In fact, Greg was the marketing vice president for a company that sold a nonfat cracker around the world. He traveled frequently, slept until noon, used what he called recreational drugs. He leaned on the door jamb. "Did you hear what I said? Stephne's the real thing. Doesn't that interest you?"

"Marginally," Jack said.

Greg blinked. He was hurt.

"It would interest me a lot more if it wasn't midnight and I didn't need a shower," Jack said. He knew that Greg found his fierce sobriety and rigid schedule quaint, a reassuring anchor in the shifting universe.

Greg buttoned his jacket, smiled a little, and said, "OK, here's the deal. Stephne and I have a chance to fly to the Nut Tree restaurant. Near Sacramento. Four of us. Her cousin Allen has a license for a Piper. We'll get a motel, have a giant breakfast, be back by noon. A lark. It'll be fun."

Jack felt oddly disappointed he wasn't asked along. He scratched the cat's ear. Sometimes he wished he'd told Greg about his life in the creek, about the time he was stabbed and left for dead, about the nights he slept barefoot with his boot laces tied around his neck so he'd have footwear in the morning. Then Greg would realize he was someone to be reckoned with. He said, "Son, you have my permission to fuck the girl and fly anywhere you want." A pause. "But be sure you're safe, ah, with her. I'm just getting to like you."

Greg gave a half laugh. "You mean, use a condom?"

Jack nodded, feeling foolish, his tenderness being pushed back at him. Irritably he picked up the newspaper from the floor.

"That's great. That you said that!" Greg grinned. He ran his hand down his tie, adding primly, "Yes, Mother, I'll be careful." Then he took one step into the room and cleared his throat. "I mean, will you baby-sit? I've got Eli this weekend and Deanna has a stroke if I don't keep the kid every second she's given me."

Sweat ran down Jack's face. Dark-haired Eli, his grandson, had Jack's own straight nose and blinking eyes. He'd met the boy once and had felt as if a part of himself had gotten loose in the world. He needed to recapture it somehow—Eli made him feel big, dangerous. The boy's very face moved him almost to tears. He couldn't tell if Eli wanted something from him or if all five-year-olds looked half-finished, needy. He'd given him a quarter. Eli had looked at it and said, "Next time, *I'll* give *you* two quarters," and Jack hadn't known if he was being mocked by a baby or not. He'd hoped for a long time that Greg would bring him around again.

"Sure," he said to his son, trying to sound offhand, though the glow of being asked to guard the child rose in him like the summer moon he'd seen outside. "But I doubt a kid would like it here. Dinky TV. Nothing fun."

"A kid would love it here! Watching people on the street from the bedroom window. The bathtub with legs. The plants. The kitchen with all the utensils."

Jack hadn't realized that Greg had observed his apartment so closely.

"Plus, there's you." Greg took his arm.

"Oh yes, the main attraction."

"You really shouldn't shift what I say like that. It shows a lack of self-esteem."

Jack rolled his eyes. He hated Greg's directness. And he could hardly think. Eli here! What would the boy eat? Where would he sit? Not in the big ugly chair or the flowered futon that smelled like cat no matter how often he blotted it with Woolite foam.

Eli was asleep in the backseat of Greg's black Porsche. Jack peered in, conscious of his every movement. Eli's blue-black eyelashes fringed pale skin; his lips were parted and he was very still. Was he breathing? The girl in front turned so that Jack could see the top of a breast spilling out over her tank top. She whispered, "He sleeps like he's dead. You could drop a building on him and he wouldn't wake up."

"I wasn't planning to drop a building on him," Jack whispered back.

She giggled, then quickly muffled the sound with her hand.

"I'll carry him up," Greg said. He lifted a backpack with a stop sign printed on it from the car floor.

"I can," said Jack, and he opened the door and slid his hand behind the boy and felt the heavy warmth of him. He took the strap of the backpack in his fingers and climbed the steps, feeling like a man bearing his bride.

Greg stayed below, calling up the stairs, "You shouldn't have any trouble with him. He can be a handful, but he's bright. Very bright!"

Jack said, "Are you missing him already?"

For a moment there was no answer. Then Greg said softly, "Maybe so. I don't know what I feel about him."

He wouldn't take him back, would he? Quickly Jack said, "Go. Have a good time. We'll be OK." He turned. I could be a beast carrying his prey, he thought.

At the top of the stairs he remembered following his father from the family grocery in Fresno up to their second-floor apartment. As they rose, the heavy meat smell of his mother's cooking would thicken. Waiting for dinner, his father would sit on the daybed in Jack's room and make Jack play hearts or Monopoly. Every so often he'd flick a hand across Jack's face or shoulder just because he was getting drunk on an empty stomach, or because he was mad at a vegetable broker, or for no reason. Jack wasn't allowed to fight back. When the grocery got closer to failing, the punches came harder. Once, Jack flared up and stomped his boot heel on his father's stockinged foot and the man knocked him cold.

The boy stirred in Jack's arms, and Jack's heart twisted. He turned to call Greg back, but the car door closed and there was an engine roar, then silence.

The child's warmth seemed to spread, burning Jack's chest. He had to put him down. Not drop him. Jack half ran into the apartment and lay the boy on his waterbed. Eli's body swayed with the little wave of the mattress, making Jack uneasy. He raised the boy up by the armpits onto the pillow and felt as if he were moving his own young self in sleep.

For a while he stood over the boy and realized he was praying. Please God, please God, please God. He didn't know what the prayer meant. A fresh breeze from the bay touched Jack's face, drying the sweat.

He went to the front room and sank into the futon. Ferris climbed up and began to knead his thigh. The shadowy room seemed filled with wind. In Fresno, the breezes pulled along the smell of stale water and a chemical odor from the cotton fields. Jack had been a teenager the last time he'd seen his father. The man had accused him of cheating. Monopoly money lay spread on the bed. "You took money from the bank when I went to the bathroom."

"I didn't." He'd only grabbed a few of the play twenties.

The back of his father's hand hit his right ear. "Don't," Jack said.

Another slap. Jack saw the black hairs on the large sausage fingers. He seized the Monopoly board and shoved it into the broad chest in front of him.

His father stood up. "So," he said, his forehead gleaming, and Jack realized his father wanted him to fight.

His stomach went cold. He kneeled by the metal frame of the bed, his hands over his head, the civil-defense posture he'd learned in school.

"Good God," his father said. He slapped Jack's back. Again. "Stand up!" Again.

Stiffening for each blow, Jack took the pain and pressed it out his spine. His father started punching with his fist, making Jack's kidneys ache. His shins were being pounded into the floor. His head was coming off. He got up on one knee and threw the bedcover over his father. The man punched at the blanket, roaring, careening around the room.

Jack followed, hitting his father in the stomach with all his might whenever he got a chance.

Finally, his father threw off the blanket, grabbed Jack's wrist, and held it as he slammed his elbow into Jack's heart.

Twisting, Jack seized his father's pumping forearm. His glance raked the room: his mother in the doorway, her hands palms up, fear pulling her face sideways at the same angle as his own. Her tension fueled him. He pushed his father against the wall and gripped the man's arm and shoulder; they struggled, each trying to break free and get in another punch. Jack wanted to shout but couldn't spare the breath. His teeth were clenched. His teeth were cracking! He looked into the purple shadows of his father's wrinkled eyes and felt himself start to ebb. No, he thought, and found another wave of strength, but it gave out faster than the first. He had nothing left. Yet there was something. For one long second neither man could move. Then Jack felt his strength rise a fraction over his father's, bending the earth on its axis. Jack was fifteen years old. He held his father's arm against the wall, then shoved the man's fingers back until there was the faint sound of bones cracking. Jack let go, turned his back, and walked slowly past his mother.

Eli came out of the bedroom at 5:00 A.M. and Jack realized the boy had slept in his miniature polo shirt and chinos, now rumpled. A sense of failure came over him. "Hi," he said. The cat in his arms lifted her head.

"Who are you?"

"Grandpa. Didn't Greg tell you?"

"No." The boy's lips were full, shiny, and his hair curved into his eyes, which looked black in the dim light.

The sorrow on his smooth face was more than Jack could bear. "You were asleep."

"I was in the car," he said firmly.

Jack said, "I carried you up here." For all the boy knew, he'd been dropped off with a stranger. Give him time, Jack told himself, his throat tight. Give him room, let him ease into this. He said carefully, "You remember me. We had a bagel downstairs with your father a while ago."

The boy's eyes widened slightly. "I don't like bagels."

"Know something? Neither do I. Usually I cook for myself."

"Good for you," Eli said.

Again, Jack didn't know if he was being mocked. He said, "That's a pretty grown-up thing to say."

The boy nodded. The cat jumped out of Jack's arms and rubbed against the boy's leg. "I don't like cats," he said, kicking Ferris, who bounded into the kitchen, yowling.

Rage rose so fast it seemed to lift Jack up from the futon. He seized the boy by the shoulders and said, "Oh no you don't!" He picked Eli up and stumbled with him to the bedroom. Jack looked at the terrified face, the open mouth with its pink, fragile tongue. Such a white neck. Jack could lean forward and bite it. No, he'd crush the little chin with his fingers. He'd—

He stopped beside the waterbed and let go. The startled boy dropped to his feet. Jack pivoted out the door, slammed it, and stood trembling on the other side.

For a second he felt blank. He hadn't hurt the child. Not even a little. Not a scratch. He sank to the floor, his back to the wall. How had the boy escaped injury? Jack didn't know. He was filled with a kind of ecstasy, a sharpening of the senses. He said as normally as possible through the door, "You can't be nasty to the cat." He saw his own quiet hand on his knee, the long fingers with knobby knuckles. He said, "You have to brush your teeth. Your backpack's beside your bed. Get your toothbrush."

A brave little voice came through the wood. "I have to do it in the bathroom. Let me out."

The boy believed Jack wouldn't hurt him. Jack knelt on the floor, too shaken to get up. He felt like he'd landed in a new country. He reached up, opened the door, and put his arms around the boy.

Eli stiffened, his hands at his sides. "I don't remember one thing about you."

Jack said, "Well, that's OK. I don't either."

Rolling his eyes, the boy walked past Jack into the bathroom.

He made eggs Benedict and Eli ate eagerly. "I want to be a chef when I grow up," he said. He sat on the stool while Jack sat beside him on the plastic yard chair he'd gotten at a garage sale.

"What are you going to cook?" He felt the boy's body beside him, tight with life.

"Lobsters. They scream when you put them in the water. My mom says so, even though you can't hear them."

"You like that screaming?"

"Not usually." The boy frowned. "Today I like that screaming. Usually I have a hamburger." Eli's talk had its own logic, like the ravings of someone in the creek, but there was no meanness in it.

"We'll go for a walk," Jack said, feeling breathless. "When we get back, your father should be here."

Eli nodded. But when it was time to go, he wouldn't put on his sandals. Then, as they got outside, Eli said he was too hot. He'd wait on the steps.

They'd just go a little way, Jack said. He knew he had to exercise, to feel his legs charging through the air and get his blood pumping, but the boy moved slowly, pulling back whenever Jack tried to up the pace. At the stores, Eli wanted to buy a new sofa for his room, a tambourine, a dog leash. Jack took his wrist and dragged him away from the pet shop. "I'll buy you a dog leash and put you on it!" he said, trying to joke.

"OK! Put me on the leash. Put me on the leash!" Eli gave a wily smile. A passing woman in a linen suit slowed her walk and watched them.

"He's just kidding," Jack said.

"I'm not!" Eli yelled. "Put me on the leash, you." He threw his arms around Jack and started licking Jack's belt.

"Stop this!" Jack said, trying to pull the boy off him.

The woman paused, considered.

Jack imagined the police handcuffing him while the boy licked his knees. "It's just a little game," he said to the woman. He felt doomed. In a second his new life would be over.

She shook her head, hugged her briefcase, and watched, a good citizen about to intervene.

"Ick! Yucky leather!" Eli stood back and raised his little eyebrows at Jack. The woman smiled and walked away, glancing back every so often.

Jack was saved. He wanted to giggle. Sunlight danced off the metal edge of the pet shop window, dazzling him. He took a breath and Eli waited until they moved on. For about ten glorious minutes the boy stayed beside him, his hand in Jack's, his hot little hand that was the whole world.

At the edge of town, they turned toward the creek. Jack lifted Eli onto his shoulders. His heart quickened as he approached the trestle. He felt like he was about to perform a high-wire act, crossing the creek with blood kin on his shoulders.

"No. No! No!" Eli shouted, pounding his shoes into Jack's chest. Jack stopped on the grassy path. An overturned Safeway cart spilled empty Coke cans down the bank.

Eli threw himself from side to side. Lurching, Jack said as calmly as possible, "It's pretty over there. I used to camp in the creek. Let me show you." His ribs were bruised. How could such a little boy have such big feet?

"I won't! No! Don't carry me across!"

There were gray forms in the creek. Were they boulders? He was about to fall onto them. "OK!" Jack shouted to the boy. "Stop!"

Instead, Eli flipped backward so his head bumped the small of Jack's back. For a second, Jack lost his balance and almost pitched to the side, but he caught himself and sank to his knees.

The boy lay dangling against his back, panting. Bent, Jack held the small thighs and wondered what to do.

"I don't want to go across," Eli said. "Take me down into the creek. Camping. Like you do."

Jack shivered in the warmth. "I don't camp anymore. It's not safe." His shoulders ached from the squirming boy.

"It is safe!" Eli whined. "There's no water. You're just saying that. I want to go camping!"

He didn't try to sit up or get down, as if dangling was his normal posture. Jack wondered if blood was rushing into Eli's face, making his cheeks ache. He tried to change the subject. "Are you a Boy Scout?"

"Jerzy's a Boy Scout. He said he'd take me camping but he didn't!"

"Well, you'll have to wait for Jerzy," Jack said. "I don't have a tent. Who's Jerzy?" His eyeballs felt compressed.

Not answering, the boy released the grip of his legs around Jack's neck and slid to the grass, where he lay on his back. "I don't have a tent either," he said with disgust.

Jack lay on his back beside him. The blue sky was covered with a high white film of clouds. Jack said quietly, "Do you do things like this to your mother?"

Silence. Then, "She plays tennis and sleeps. But I can wake her up whenever I want. She says it's OK. I let Jerzy wake her up usually."

Jack imagined a silent house with a tanned woman in white clothes sleeping heavily on the couch. Her talent for sleeping had been passed on to Eli. Poor kid, thought Jack, heavy sleep combined with my nerves. He stood up, a wave of unnamed sadness welling in his throat.

The boy stood up too. Jack took his hand. They walked toward home.

He thought of the time he'd had the flu and spent five days under a bush near the trestle. Delirious, he thought he was the bush, sticky with sap and ants. He licked rainwater off the leaves. Then, one morning, his head and stomach felt better, but he was profoundly sad. Why? He didn't know. He lay under the branches that brushed sunlight across his face and realized that his life—the chair by the periodicals in the warm Newell branch library, stale maple bars at Safeway every Friday at 3:00 A.M., the mashed-potato-and-floor-wax smell of the basement in the Presbyterian ministry where he usually ate lunch—no longer appealed to him. Somehow, with instinct and luck, he'd made a life in the creek, but now he wanted something else. Three days later, he walked into Floral Magic with their Help Wanted sign in his hand and said he had lots of experience cleaning up, he'd done it for years at his father's store. The harassed wife of the owner handed him a bottle of Glass Wax and told him the display cases hadn't been cleaned since their one employee quit showing up a month ago.

Eli perked up as they got closer to home. He chattered about Mighty Morphin Power Rangers, which Jack figured was a TV show about white blood cells or drug lords. The boy dawdled, danced, barked.

By the time they returned to the apartment, Jack was exhausted. He slumped in his chair and turned on the TV—a cooking show. Eli crawled into his lap. Together they watched the Galloping Gourmet make lamb chops and escargots. Eli sat with eyes wide, body tense. Jack dozed.

At one o'clock, Jack realized he was hungry. Eli hadn't moved from his lap. No Greg. Jack kissed the boy, went into the kitchen and made tomato sandwiches for lunch, and they sat on the floor and watched Julia Child cook fillet of sole. She patted the fish, her man-size hands loving the feel of its flesh. Greg would come soon and Jack could go for his long Saturday run.

Eli stared at the TV, his legs crossed, his lips slightly open. A kind of expectancy radiated from him, filling the room, making Jack feel like something was about to happen. He had to be very careful now. Just hang in there for a few more minutes and Greg would come for the boy or call. The black phone sat on the end table, its long cord snaking across the room.

Twenty minutes, twenty-five. Julia Child, looking tired, with her hair dangling across her broad forehead, fingered new potatoes and hoarsely yelled about the virtues of paprika.

Eli said, "My mom's in Hawaii."

"I thought she lived in San Francisco." Jack could call there. Get her to take the boy. Julia Child sprinkled lemon juice over the fish as if baptizing it.

"She does. She got married yesterday. She's watching the moon in Hawaii. With Jerzy. Jerzy's funny."

"Funny ha ha or funny weird?"

A frown. "The moon's bigger in Hawaii. And it's red. I think the volcanoes make it red." He paused for a moment, as if stricken. "My dad's supposed to keep me for two weeks."

"Two weeks?" Greg had run away! Julia Child left the kitchen muttering and the camera panned across a succulent fish bordered with red potatoes.

Eli's lips had lost their shine and there were purple shadows under his cheeks. Had he instantly starved? He said, "At Christmas, he left me at the neighbor's for four nights and five days. My mom was mad. But I like daddy's neighbor. He squeezes oil from orange skins and burns it with his lighter. Fff-ttt!" He stood up and started to hop on one leg.

So! Greg would dump his son on anybody. A pyromaniac. A grandpa. What difference? Jack felt hollow. He'd show Greg and keep Eli—forever. No, he couldn't do that. The boy would wear him out. He'd collapse. He couldn't even take another hour of this. What was he thinking? Don't let up now. Don't let your heart explode. You'll get past this.

Somehow he had to get back to his old quiet life. How he longed for a silent, fast jog. The saliva in his mouth was metallic—he could almost taste the run.

Carefully he said to the bouncing boy, "What's your mother's number?"

"I told you," Eli screamed. "She's in Hawaii!"

"We'll leave her a message. And she'll check her messages and send somebody." Who would it be?

Abruptly, wordlessly, Eli sank to the floor, crossed his legs, and put his chin in his hands. He stared at the TV. The program had changed to news. There was a picture of a house going up in flames.

Jack found a kids' channel. The Morphins—teenagers in pastel motorcycle helmets—were using karate kicks on monsters. Jack sat in his chair and waited for Eli to recover. How long would the silence last?

Through the afternoon and into the evening, Eli didn't talk. Jack tried to read the newspaper, do the crossword puzzle. The cat slept beside him. Finally, when the window in the kitchen alcove was black with the night, he said, "I think your father's coming soon."

Cartoons were back on. Eli didn't move.

"Let's not make this harder than it is," Jack said.

Silence.

Jack stared at the almost-empty grid of the crossword. Usually he was good with words. He'd aced the GED test sometime during his first years in San Francisco, when he was a bike messenger. His eyes blurred. He'd have to move soon or he'd die. He made himself doze, a trick he'd learned sleeping out on cold nights. He was flying down the creek like Luke Skywalker, the banks just inches from the tips of his wings. He was in control, guided by a force.

Eli said, "I think it's 655-1263."

Half asleep, Jack wrote the numbers on the newspaper. He brought himself to full consciousness, then called Eli's mother. The voice on the machine was crisp.

The boy watched, his face white, pink blotches along the jawbone. He put his hands on his little knees and said, "When I leave here, I want the cat."

Careful now, careful. Jack left his number and put down the phone. He said, "I didn't think you liked her."

"Maybe I'd be nice to her if you were dead."

Jack held his breath, let it out. "How about if you and I go to Burger King for a hamburger? When we get back, your dad will probably be here. Or your mom'll call."

"I'm not hungry." Watching Jack, Eli took off his sandals. No walking.

A spark of panic flared in Jack's chest. He couldn't stay cooped up.

"*Kids* don't die," Eli said. He had a lonely look.

"Not if they go out with their grandpa and eat their dinner," Jack said evenly.

Abruptly Eli stood up and jumped on the futon, bouncing the cat off. She squawked and hid behind the philodendron. "I'm not leaving this house. Not ever!" Eli screamed. "We can get takeout until we die. I like Chinese!" The wood frame creaked. It was the first piece of furniture Jack had ever bought.

Grabbing the boy's knees, he wrestled him to the cushion. "OK," he shouted. Miraculously, his hands held the boy's warm skinniness lightly. Jack's mind roared, but he said calmly, as if using someone else's voice, "Why don't we put you to bed. If you wait for something to happen, it never does."

He had to get rid of the boy for a while, clear his head, regain a sense of movement.

Eli blinked. His little nostrils flared. "I'll brush my teeth," he said, and he left the room.

Panting, Jack fell back on the futon. He felt stiff from knowing he couldn't run tonight. He needed to feel the night wind stir him up, but it wouldn't come if he didn't open the window. He couldn't. A stupor held him down.

Two hours later, he forced himself to rise. He pushed up the window over the kitchen sink and gulped cold air. The cat slid against his ankle. He went into the bedroom, where Eli lay crosswise in blue pajamas with piping. He opened that window, too, then covered the boy. Feeling as if he were in slow motion, he kicked the cat out of the way.

He had to leave. Feel the sharp wind against his chest. Run the edge. Eli would be all right—he had to be. You shouldn't leave a child unguarded. He had to leave this child.

Slowly he pulled on his tights. He checked on the boy again. Motionless. From on top of the refrigerator he took the key to the outside door. It felt greasy. He went down the stairs and made sure the door locked.

Finally he was moving. The tension in his legs and stomach eased but his mind pounced on vague worries. What if the building burned down? What if someone broke in? He ran faster and faster. Nothing was going to happen.

He did his creek route, then crossed the overpass and ran on the other side of 101, East Palo Alto. Here the houses seemed to sag with the weight of the rusted cars on their front lawns. There were bars on the windows, chunks of broken concrete in piles at an empty lot. The moon was a curled piece of metal. He was a sweat machine going at the speed of light. He turned back home.

Suddenly he remembered Eli's grandmother. That woman he'd slept with when he was a different person. Her name was Susan. That night, she'd had on something with red buttons. She was in his tissues, and now that he'd been emptied out he could feel her. Her ribs against his. Her hand brushing his ear. She had silky black brows, like Eli's.

Gasping, he slowed to a walk. He was almost home. He didn't plan to find her or even think about her much, but he shook to find out that all this time she'd been waiting in his blood. He'd never get rid of her or of anybody he'd touched.

There was a scream from his apartment, then another. Irrationally, he wondered if this was what he'd been expecting all his life. He fished for the key in his pocket, but it slipped from his wet hand, clanking to the sidewalk. He picked it up, only his hand shook too hard to find the lock. The screams were louder.

Now the key was too big to fit. He distinctly heard Eli's voice swollen with fear. "Don't! No! Don't!"

Finally the lock gave. Jack ran up the steps, miraculously opened the apartment door on the first try, and pushed into the room shoulder first, ready for any thug.

Nobody.

He raced into the bedroom. Eli was sitting up and pointing at Jack. "Don't!" he yelled. "Stop! Stop! No!"

Jack took a step toward the boy. "It's me. Grandpa."

Eli grabbed a pillow and batted the air, a madman in little boy's pajamas. His mouth was twisted down.

Jack had stepped into his nightmare. "It's me," he whispered urgently. "You know me. Grandpa."

The boy batted the air harder. "Stay away! Don't kill me! Stop!"

"I'm not going to kill you."

"Stop! Stop!"

Jack slammed the bedroom window shut. A man in a suit looked up from the street. The woman on his arm pulled a portable phone from her purse. She was going to call the police. If they came, Eli might say he didn't know a thing about this man who said he was Grandpa. Jack would go to jail. Eli would be left with strangers. Jack hissed, "You *have* to be quiet."

Eli gave a shriek and crawled to the far corner of the bed, his feet tangled in the sheets. Jack grabbed one leg and pulled him closer.

"Don't touch me!" Eli yelled.

Jack ran to the bathroom, drenched a towel in icy water, came back and threw it at the boy.

Eli batted it away, opened his eyes wide, then raised up his little hands. In an instant he was conscious, cold and bewildered.

"You were dreaming." Cautiously Jack came toward him.

"Grandpa!" His mouth hung open and he seemed dazed. In his lap was the wet towel.

"You were dreaming," Jack repeated.

"No." Eli said, "I don't have those dreams anymore. I'm grown-up."

Relief that the boy made sense spread through Jack; then came gutting disappointment. He sat on the bed. He'd thought

Eli was fearless, but no, the fear lay just under his skin. He was just like Jack, only younger. The boy was a damp, shivering bundle in his arms.

The phone rang. Feeling doomed, Jack went to the front room and answered mechanically.

"Is Eli still there? This is his mother. Could I talk to him?" The clipped voice had risen with panic.

For a moment Jack thought she'd heard Eli screaming just before. "Where are you?" he said.

"He's OK, isn't he? Greg said you were a nice guy. Is he upset? I'm sorry I'm crying. I just got your message. We're in Los Angeles. Jerzy's trying to get a flight back. It's all my fault. I knew Greg would pull something like this. Oh my God. He must be asleep. The way he sleeps, you'll never wake him up. I'm babbling, aren't I?"

Jack said, "Not really. I can understand you." He was still trying to believe she wasn't a cop. "I'll get Eli."

Instantly the boy was at his elbow, grabbing the phone. "Mom! Did you swim in the ocean? No. I'm OK. We're living on top of a restaurant. My bedroom smells like eggs. Tomorrow! Where's Jerzy? I can't hear you. Tomorrow! I love you too."

The boy who put down the phone and turned back to Jack was transformed—seconds before, he'd been a terrified mouse; now his cheeks were full and cherubic, his eyes steady, the lids shiny.

"She's coming! Jerzy got the ticket while she was on the phone. Seven-twenty tomorrow!" He pumped his fist.

He can't be that happy, Jack thought. One second I'm all he's got. The next he's gone. His head ached, as if he'd pounded it on something.

Eli danced. "She had to go to Los Angeles to get the plane to Hawaii. The plane needed fixing! She got my message!"

Jack felt papery, as if he and the sidewalk below could be crumpled into a ball. He said, "OK. Let's go camping. It'll kill a few hours while we wait for your mom. You can smell the grass while you sleep. I'll be your bodyguard."

Eli said disgustedly, "You don't know how to camp."

Desperate, Jack said, "I know how to camp better than Jerzy."

"You don't have a tent."

"See, I know how to camp without a tent."

Eli gave a little smile, then the smile vanished. "We'll be back before she comes."

"Yes. I'll keep track."

With a kitchen knife Jack slit a large garbage bag and spread the plastic on the dusty ground. Eucalyptus trees towered into the night sky, reeking of their medicine smell. A few yards away, Eli stood in front of a stone angel that was praying for Leland and Jane Stanford's souls. He watched Jack's preparations keenly.

Jack had decided Stanford land was the safest place to camp—not too many cops, no midnight sprinklers like in the city parks, no peeking neighbors or vicious stray dogs. The creek with its men battling demons was a mile away.

He laid a folded blanket over the plastic and said, "Your bed, Mon-sewer." He could hardly talk.

Eli sat straight-backed and smiling.

Jack had forgotten how to smile. He used the knife to spread peanut butter on a Hi Ho cracker. He figured fires weren't allowed among the peeling, decrepit eucalyptus trees, and besides, he didn't want to draw attention to himself. What he wanted to do was go to sleep and not wake up. Tomorrow he'd have his life back. What life? Maybe he'd call in sick on Monday. Rest. Take a break from Floral Magic, the measly tips, the complaints when lilies were bruised, the tin can of a truck he had to drive.

He put a cracker on top of the peanut butter and handed the sandwich to Eli. "Our midnight snack."

The boy ate one after another, as fast as Jack could make them. "What was your nightmare about?" Jack asked.

"Nothing."

"Black nothing or red nothing?"

Eli didn't smile. "I don't have nightmares anymore. I told you." He laid his head against Jack's upper arm as naturally as if he'd been doing it for years.

Jack's mind stopped. His blood seemed to gather at the spot where Eli's ear lightly touched his shirt. He was staked to the ground by that touch. Carefully he lifted his arm so Eli's head rested against his chest. He put his hand on the angle of Eli's elbow and the boy snuggled closer. Tonight, thought Jack, tonight I'll be his pillow. There was a glow behind the distant red roofs of Stanford's main campus. Maybe the moon was rising.

"My mother says I'm too old for nightmares," Eli said. "They come when your brain's growing up from being a baby."

"You're not a baby, that's for sure," Jack said softly. Their shadow lay beside them.

Jack felt the boy's cheek move into a smile against his ribs. "If I had a dream, I'd dream you ate me."

Startled, feeling like the trees were listening, Jack said, "I'd like to eat you, but who would I talk to then?"

Eli took that in, pulled the blanket over his legs. He said, "Is it going to be cold tonight?"

Was it going to be cold? Jack felt like a god rocked by his subjects' utter faith. He whispered, "No. Not cold."

Soon, the boy lay still. Jack became aware of his own breath, the smell of peanut butter, dry earth. Time passed—a half hour, maybe an hour.

There was a rustle in the distance. The crackling sound came closer. Someone coming. Jack's heart pitched forward. Most good people were in bed this time of night. Alone, Jack would have run, but with Eli here he needed to defend himself. Where was the knife? Lying clean in the empty cracker box four feet away. He couldn't get it without making a noise. Besides, it wasn't much more than a butter knife.

To his left was a thick branch. He leaned over on his back and grasped it. Eli's head was on his stomach. Jack waited. Who was the intruder? Someone from the creek looking for trouble? After Stanford football games at the stadium, some of the guys came for empty soda cans and the dregs in beer bottles. Jack had done it himself. Once he'd gotten so drunk and lost in the trees that he'd sat down and cried.

There—a boy and a girl walking. Teenagers, maybe older. They had on baggy shorts and T-shirts. Jack eased his grip on the stick. The boy had his hand on her neck and she was giggling. Without seeing Jack, they stopped by the statue. The boy's hair flopped into his face as he leaned against the carved stone, kissed her. Jack saw his hands disappear under her shirt. The kids had no idea anyone was close enough to throw a rock at them. They muttered to each other. Jack couldn't hear. What would students say to each other? Jack couldn't imagine—just like they couldn't imagine men creeping through the night, men who could explode at any minute.

Their murmuring went on and on. Jack dozed in the weeds, then opened his eyes. The students had slid themselves to the ground. Their soft sounds were part of the whispering breeze. Eli slept with his head on the notch of Jack's ribs. The moon lay on its back. Dew sorted itself from the night air and brought a freshness to Jack's lips. Suddenly he knew what the college boy was thinking: Tonight, I got lucky. Jack smiled. Eli's breath touched his arm. All night Jack didn't move. He was safe.

Only the
Lonely Heart

I'm a sales associate at Nordstrom in the petites department, but I should have been an actress. Last summer, I took a drama class at San Francisco State and my professor, Olen Sherr, who always wore the same black T-shirt and loafers, said I was good at creating personalities. I know how people tick and can make their style my own.

As long as they're characters on stage or customers in the store. I lose my power with flesh-and-blood men, especially when they move into my rented house near the zoo. Though I'm quick to learn their moods and their tastes in food and sex, their deeper wishes remain a mystery to me. No matter how well I please them, eventually they find someone else, or discover they have to climb Mount Aconcagua, or just leave.

When Olen came to live with me, I put a large poster of a David Hockney stage set over my bed. He loved it. Storming out six months later, his clothes piled high in his open MG, he yelled, "You know what your problem is, Catherine? You're too nice. You make everyone else feel like a jerk." I thought about that for weeks, trying to locate my failure.

This last winter, the California rains never stopped. By January, whole fields of strawberries and artichokes were underwater; the *Chronicle* ran pictures of freeway bridges collapsing, cars flying across the chasm. I hunkered down and poured myself into my work while I waited for love.

Selling comes easily to me; I could get women to buy bikinis in Alaska, or in wet San Francisco, for that matter. I'm the top producer on Nordstrom's second floor in Stonestown Mall. My secret is that I'm a chameleon, an actress on the job. I watch my customer closely and imitate the movements of her soul, so to speak. In a few seconds, I almost become her. If she tilts her head just so, indicating that her thoughts are heavy and she needs something new to lift her spirits, I tilt my head also. I need something new, too, someone new to talk to—her. I smile at the moment she looks up. Then I show her the *très cher* silk blouse with the beautiful hand. She says, "The perfect thing! How did you know?"

I love the hunt, the thrill of moving in on a customer and clearing away her doubts about cloth and zippers and buttons, the little things that might in some small but important way define her. An aficionado of creating and re-creating image, I never cling stubbornly to one style, and my customers appreciate that. But then there's the long-haired woman in Birkenstocks who breezes between the carousels, barely glancing at the clothes. She's much too busy and discriminating to be fooled by fashion trends. She isn't even sure why she's shopping when she could be working on a screenplay or getting a medical degree. I let my eyes rake carelessly across the store to let her know that I'm not exactly sure why I'm here either. I stare into space, thinking of Goethe. When she's trying to decide between two blouses, I say, "Do you want to see those in natural light? The window's by the elevator." Away from the fluorescence that gives everything a pinkish tinge, I show her the difference between ecru and beige. So relieved is she to find someone who understands that the store's very light is artificial, misleading, she buys both pieces.

Carson Faranacci showed up in my department just after the January white sale. He held his umbrella forlornly between his legs while I checked on a customer in the dressing room, then he asked for ladies' gloves. They were downstairs. Sensing that he needed someone to joke with, I said, "You don't want gloves. Either go to lingerie and get her something black or dump her."

Eyebrows lifted, he thought for a minute. His rain-damp suit hung limply at the thighs. Its faint smell of wool livened the air, making me feel alert to the slope of his shoulders, the athletic ease of his stance. I leaned in front of the counter at the same angle as his lucky umbrella.

His face relaxed as he said, "I'll bet they didn't teach you to say that in salesperson school."

I smiled, my heart beating faster. "So I should be complimenting you on that tie, I suppose?"

He looked down and lifted the end. "You don't like balloons?" A frowning pause. "She got me this tie."

I shook my head sorrowfully and he laughed.

Carson and I began to spend long evenings walking the foggy beach below the Cliff House. The sand was cold and stiff under our bare feet as we talked. At forty, Carson was five years older than I. After meeting me, he'd finally quit seeing the stockbroker he'd almost married. She wanted children and he didn't. He'd been married young, he said, and already had a seventeen-year-old son, who lived with the ex-wife in Salt Lake City. She had become a Mormon and their son was rebelling.

I wondered how someone could leave his own son rebelling in Utah, but Carson needed to travel frequently, mostly to Japan and Indonesia, where he sold used computers. He wanted to make a pile in ten years and retire. Then he was going to ride a bike around the world.

One evening I turned to him in the mist and told him about my short-lived drama career. Maybe I was trying to make my life sound as exciting as his. I told him I understood people and could play them. I gave him my impression of Elizabeth Taylor impersonating Clint Eastwood—"Make me, daily!" says Elizabeth as she rides sidesaddle into the sunset.

Carson kissed me and pulled me down behind a sand dune to shelter us from the wind.

Within weeks, he was practically living with me between business trips. I learned to make the focaccia bread with olive oil and rosemary that he loved. I took down the Hockney poster and painted my bedroom sky blue, a color that made him feel free, he said. I figured I'd learn to like it eventually.

By Presidents' Day his son, Geoffrey, had moved into my guest room. His mother had kicked him out and Carson said the boy needed a place to stay while he tried to get into Lowell High in San Francisco. Geoffrey made me uneasy, probably because he was the incarnation of his father, with the same straight nose and clear gray eyes. In an outsize flannel shirt and large jeans he looked like he must have been three sizes bigger when he'd gone shopping. Did he have a body inside those limp clothes? The idea of living with my lover's son didn't appeal to me, but I let Geoffrey stay anyway. I didn't use the front bedroom and figured Carson would come around more often with his son at my place.

In fact, soon after Geoffrey arrived Carson's travel schedule got more hectic. And I hardly saw Geoffrey. He'd be asleep when I left for work. At night, I'd think I heard his combat boots in the entryway. He got into Lowell but told his father that he needed time to find an apartment. He didn't seem to study or even to own books. It was like living with a ghost. He left half-eaten sandwiches in my living room. Once I told Carson I felt half-eaten myself. He laughed and said, "It's only temporary," then went off to Hong Kong.

Early one morning, a teenage girl showed up at my door and announced that she was Geoffrey's girlfriend. Most women dress for other women; a few, like me, dress for men. This one apparently dressed for her cat. Despite the rain she had on ballet-type shoes and a tobacco-colored sweater too short for her leggings, which bagged at the knees.

I said, "Geoffrey's not here right now." I wasn't sure he'd been home at all that night.

"I'll wait," she said, giving a little shake of her head. She devoted all her sense of style to the neck up. Her shiny hair rippled; her lips were perfect peach, her eyebrows arched.

"No," I said. "I have to leave for work."

"Please. I just came from Salt Lake." She paused and straightened her small shoulders.

I wondered if there was a bruise under the ivory makeup at the outer corner of her eye. I decided it was just the gray morning light.

As if joining a self-help group, she said, "I'm Tina and I'm pregnant." Another pause. "And I'm tired. I took a bus."

I felt a rivulet of panic. "I really can't handle another person living in my house that I don't know."

She frowned. "I don't plan to live here."

A gust of wind brushed cold across my face. She looked chilled, too, with bluish shadows hollowing her cheeks. I said, "I'm sorry. Come in. Please. You must be exhausted."

In the living room, I brought her a cup of Earl Grey. We talked. She'd been with Geoffrey for two months in Salt Lake, but she'd broken it off when she found out about the pregnancy. She hadn't wanted to tell him. "He has a temper and I wasn't sure about living with him long-term. I had to think about it. He went berserk when I said he couldn't see me and I didn't tell him why." She smiled, rolled her eyes. "He pulled out his mother's rosebushes with his bare hands! Think about it. She said I was trash, and he did that for me. His hands were bloody! I love him. How could I not know that?"

I felt defenseless against her story.

She tilted her head and said, "He's such a good person really. He just gets mad. It started when he was a little guy. His father would pick him up for summer visitation, leave him with friends for a few hours, then not come back for days. I think Geoffrey's still ticked off, even though he says you can't carry on about when you were a baby. If I love him, I can't just take part of him, can I? I have to take him and his temper. Help him with it. I can do that, you know."

The astonishing thing was that Geoffrey had told her so much about himself. So he could speak when he wanted to. I felt better toward him. And I liked the way she said "little guy," the way she excused his anger while keeping her own position. "He's mad all the time?" I said. "He hits you?"

Her chin jerked up. "No," she said. "Not anymore. He got over that." She touched her mouth.

I felt confused, strangely moved by her, and anxious that I'd be late for work, but I smiled and said, "I can tell you haven't had breakfast. There's English muffins and grape jelly in the fridge. You look like the kind who likes jelly."

She leaned back in the chair. "Actually, I prefer peanut butter."

She'd seemed like someone who'd love clear, sweet things. I rarely misjudged women, and the small mistake heightened my sense of being vulnerable. "I've got that too," I said, feeling a kinship with her almost against my will—I preferred peanut butter also. "You can stay here today. I'll show you Geoffrey's room."

Geoffrey came home that night, and when Tina told him about the baby he took her in his arms and cried. I hadn't expected such tenderness from him. Later I could hear them murmuring in Geoffrey's room as I built a fire in the fireplace. A strange contentment came over me. The next morning, I said that Tina could stay for a few days, maybe weeks, if she needed to. They argued sometimes, but then her soft laughter would return. I was happy for them even though I didn't hear from Carson and work was slow, very slow.

One thing bothered me. I couldn't figure Tina out. In fact, the longer she stayed with me, the less I understood her. She decided to marry Geoffrey but give the baby up for adoption. He didn't like the idea and neither did I.

"But won't you want a baby someday?" I asked as I sat in the corner of a dressing room and watched her struggle into the ugliest maternity jumper I'd ever seen. She looked buckled into a balloon.

"Yes," she said dreamily. She turned in front of the mirror. Changing the subject, she said, "I like it. It makes me look like I own a Suburban. I've always wanted to be one of those moms sitting up high in traffic looking smug as hell."

She wasn't listening. I said, "I'd like something softer on you." I'd offered to buy anything she wanted, but I hadn't realized most maternity clothes came in cute and cuter.

"Well, I like this," she said. "I look like I belong to the PTA." She paused, eyed me in the mirror. "When I dropped out last fall, my dad got me a job as the cashier in a car-parts store. He made me go every day. Sometimes nobody said a thing to me except, 'Hi, honey. Do you take Visa?' For a few months I just want to look important. Is there anything wrong with that?"

"You could look important in a raw-silk sweater."

Tina held my gaze in the mirror. "You can't change my mind."

Her obstinacy scared me. She didn't examine her motives much and wasn't influenced by other people's opinions. Stubbornness was a strength I'd never have, and hers made me edgy.

Tina patted her rounded stomach and went back to our original subject. "I'm giving my baby away. It's like a gift to the world. My gift."

For a second I was rocked by the enormity of her gift, by the happiness she'd give a childless couple. And I realized that in some animal part of me I'd wanted a baby for years. Once a customer had me hold her fussy infant while she wrote a check. The child nestled against me and gently sucked my collarbone. I felt embarrassed, and awestruck by the child's determination, her readiness to love anyone, me.

What would Carson do if I decided to raise Tina's baby? Leave me, probably. He didn't want to start over again, said he'd been a lousy father the first time. But wasn't he already leaving me bit by bit? The signs were clear. I was becoming a stopover on his way to somewhere else, but I still felt bound by his likes and dislikes. As long as I loved him, his needs were mine. With a start, I realized that this might be where I had gone wrong. But how could I make myself not know what he wanted? A buzz of confusion filled my mind.

Tina was still looking at me. "Don't you want a baby someday?"

"I don't know," I said. At that moment I really didn't.

"You don't know if you want a baby?" Her sudden sarcasm surprised me. Usually she floated on the goodwill of pregnancy.

I shrugged. "It's complicated for me."

She started peeling out of the jumper very fast. "Me too," she said angrily. "I don't tell you how hard it'll be to give the baby away, but that doesn't mean I don't cry at night when Geoffrey's asleep."

I touched her shoulder, which had stayed surprisingly dainty even as her belly grew heavy. "I know you do," I said. "I hear you."

"And you do nothing about it?"

"What could I do? Geoffrey's there." I felt falsely accused.

She raised her hands in exasperation, then turned back to the mirror. Pulling on pants with an enormous elastic panel in front, she said, "I can tell you this. I'm going to interview people for the adoption and they're going to have to show me that they're dying to have a family. They can't be cool and wishy-washy."

Again, I felt implicated. Cool and wishy-washy. Was that how she saw me? No, surely she was talking about the adoptive family.

"I don't want to fight," I said.

She nodded sadly. "I know."

I felt like I'd said the wrong thing. What did she want?

She tried on a long blouse I'd picked.

"There," I said, "you look like Christie Brinkley."

She sniffed. "A short, fat Christie Brinkley."

"Just the look I was trying to achieve."

The next day she told me her savings were running out and she needed a job. I got her some morning hours at Nordstrom in gift wrap. She said she liked it, but I couldn't imagine why. It only paid minimum wage even if the queen of England came in to have her crown boxed. I couldn't live like that. Every blouse and skirt and silk scarf that walked out of my department gave me 6.75 percent back and the rush of another victory.

Finally the rains stopped. The sun seemed like a foreign substance streaming through my kitchen window, bouncing off the buildings of the mall. One afternoon it was really slow and my manager told me to go home. I checked out. Tina had already left and I found myself driving home fast. I'd been trying to teach her to cook and she said she wanted to learn how to make baked Alaska since that was the one thing you couldn't get delivered in the middle of the night.

The day was bright and breezy, the house cool. Tina and Geoffrey were both out. The stillness of my house was a little scary. I went into their room.

The silk sweater I'd bought Tina was draped on the window seat and the bed was unmade. I tried to imagine her life. How would it feel to have a baby under my heart and then give it away? What would it be like to ignore other people's judgments? Tina's life resisted me. Knowing people was my ace in the hole. What would be left if I lost that?

I took off my red bomber jacket and tried on the big sweater. Though I'd never seen her wear it, it smelled of distant flowers, like her. I sat on the bed she shared with Geoffrey and tried to picture sleeping with a mere boy, his combat boots on the floor. I couldn't. I pulled the sweater off over my head and found the ragged sweatshirt she usually wore around the house. Its sleeves were cut off and my arms felt strangely exposed. Their room, which was really my room, seemed bare. The white of the birch outside was too bright. A shadow passed in front of it.

Someone coming to the front door. Yes, a knock. I rose to meet it and there was Carson coming in and talking as if a full month hadn't passed since I'd heard his voice. "Oh, Catherine, I'm so glad you're here. I was just going to wait on the doorstep if you weren't." He'd loosened his tie and pushed up the sleeves of his soft suit jacket. He looked tired, his dimples running into the creases that crossed his cheeks. He came straight into the living room and stood by the fireplace full of white ash.

Reading failure on his face, I knew he needed respect. "Waiting on a doorstep doesn't sound like you," I said, giving him a cool smile even as my heart raced. How could I want him back, knowing he'd disappear at any minute?

He sighed. "Oh, I know how to twist in the wind. I've spent a month at it. The deal of a lifetime. Ha!"

Without thinking, I moved back into the front bedroom. Carson followed, and we sat on the rumpled bed.

Taking my hand, Carson said he'd planned to come home with a fistful of yen he'd make off the shipload of used computers he had waiting in Honolulu. But the deal never quite closed. The guy from Tokyo kept coming back with one more little demand.

"I thought the guy was in Hong Kong."

He shrugged. "No, Tokyo."

I tried to believe him. He stroked my hand, put it to his face as he talked. His skin was smooth and I knew he'd shaved a second time that day before coming over. Hot confusion rose in my chest.

"You want my sympathy?" I broke in.

He looked at me. "I'm sorry. I'm really sorry. I don't know why I left like that. I guess I can only see the thing right in front of my face."

It was true that Carson got caught up in the moment. That was what I liked about him.

"Did they make you eat seaweed?" I asked.

He smiled. "Oceans of seaweed."

"And squid?"

"Miles of tentacles." He put a hand to the neck of my sweatshirt, let it slide down, and said, "New look?"

"Only the clothes. Same underneath."

He got up, and I followed him down the hall to my bedroom.

At that moment, the blue seemed harsh, jarring our lovemaking into a hot stroking frenzy. Often Carson talked about my body while we touched, but today he was intensely silent. We lay together for a long time, then I rolled over. I said, "You shouldn't come around for a while. I need to think about where I'm headed."

Never before had I been the one to push away. Scared, I was aware of my nakedness.

"How long?" he asked.

"Right now I can't quantify it."

He smiled at the ceiling, then sobered. "I know I deserve this."

"It's not about you."

"Why do I believe that?"

All week, I felt like a stranger to myself. In a trance, I sold a lot of clothes. As usual, my customers told me bits of stories about themselves, their children, their boyfriends. I felt flooded with information, with other people's lives.

On Sunday I made a special dinner for Tina and Geoffrey. He'd bleached his hair white, making his dark eyebrows stand out. He and Tina were pretty quiet, and at first I wondered if they felt shy about the relative formality of eating in the dining room rather than in the breakfast nook. But no, Geoffrey was tense, unaware of his surroundings, and he held his elbows close to his body. Usually, his whole self leaned a little toward Tina. A misty sun coated the windows.

Geoffrey, a vegetarian, ate only pickles, rice, and buttered carrots, all with a spoon. Tina nibbled at the turkey breast I'd marinated all night. "So," I said, "looks like we don't need to build an ark after all."

"I never thought we did," Geoffrey said forcefully. "A lot of rain shouldn't be as scary as people make it out to be." The stud in his ear looked to me like a jade pea. I was amazed at his frowning optimism.

Tina's face tightened. "How can you say that?"

Geoffrey turned to her. "It was just rain."

"People drowned!"

Parking his used spoon on the tablecloth, Geoffrey looked at me. His nostrils flared and his lips were set in a grim line. Then he spoke. "We may as well tell you—there's not going to be any holy matrimony." He said "holy" as if it meant full of holes.

Tina's eyes got big but she didn't say anything.

He continued talking to me. "She's still giving the baby away. She says she doesn't want to start marriage with so much responsibility." He talked as if she weren't there. I could imagine Carson doing the same thing if he felt cornered. The faint blush of Geoffrey's cheeks deepened with rage and his hair seemed even whiter.

As gently as I could, I said, "Didn't you know that all along?"

"I thought she'd change her mind! The baby's living inside her. What is she, a robot?"

I wondered. How could someone leave a part of themselves behind? I said, "You and I don't know what she feels like." At least I didn't know. Nor did I understand how she could sit there in silence. Why didn't she defend herself?

Geoffrey slammed away from the table. "Well, I'm not marrying a robot. I suppose she'll leave him on somebody's doorstep with a note pinned to his shirt, 'I'm nobody's baby. Please take care of me.' "

The image horrified me too. "She wouldn't," I said. "She's already contacted a good agency." Or at least I assumed she had.

He turned back, and the sneer on his face frightened me. He said, "What do you know? I'll bet you don't even realize my father's thinking about not coming back to you."

My heart went cold but I doubted that Geoffrey really knew what his father would do. "I do realize it. We discussed it." Though not exactly like that.

Wanting to hurt, he said, "You should know that my father's a jerk."

Now I was angry. "Don't say that!" I yelled. "You shouldn't say something like that! You're his son."

His eyes cut to me. "I shouldn't say the truth just because he's my father?"

That night, Geoffrey left for a fishing trip to Mount Shasta with friends. Tina kept her door shut for two days. Was she mad at me? It was hard to imagine her staying angry, yet her silence was a nagging absence in the house.

The third morning, she sat in the kitchen drinking coffee. I said amiably, "I've read caffeine is OK after the first trimester."

She gave me a very brief smile. Then nothing.

I said irritably, "I've read that it's pleasant to talk to the person you live with."

"Good morning," she said.

I put on a pair of flowing black pants and went to work feeling empty. Now I understood the boredom of most clerks. The recession was supposed to be long over, but my customers bought basics, spending their money carefully. Didn't they realize that the economy needed extravagant buyers? That I needed buyers? There were only so many times I could rearrange linen pants. Even during a good year, California weather doesn't allow a clean seasonal break in fashion, and racks of light cotton dresses stood next to wool suits. I felt the spring chaos of my department as my own confusion and kept thinking, irrationally, "Who's in charge here?"

In fact, Geoffrey had taken charge. My manager, a grandmother with blond bangs, came to my cash register at a trot, her eyes wild. They needed me in gift wrap immediately. A boy carrying a gun was threatening an employee and wanted Catherine who worked downstairs to get his father. He was crying for Catherine! Get Catherine!

I leaped up the escalator, which seemed to have slowed, and stood in the entrance to the gift-wrap room. Tina and Geoffrey were frozen in front of the counter. He held the gun down near his thigh, but he had his face right up to hers. His cheekbone stood out in profile, his temple gleamed with sweat. She cringed, her face blotchy and her eyes on the gun. He said, "I'll ask you one more time, when did you find out it was a boy?" She didn't answer. The security lady stood by the wall saying soothingly, "Geoffrey, drop the gun. Drop the gun, Geoffrey, then we'll talk. Drop the gun."

Geoffrey hadn't seen me, but when I began to edge toward him he sensed a presence. "Dad?" he asked, his voice cracking. Without thinking, I lunged for the gun and he shrugged me off like a bear tossing away some small, bothersome animal. The gun went off, making the floor explode.

Hands on ears, Tina ducked beneath the edge of the counter. Unhurt, I scooted on my knees to the wall. The crack of the gun had galvanized Geoffrey's fury and made him calm. As feeling drained from him, he turned marble white, bloodless, and steadily leveled the gun in Tina's trembling face. Even her stomach seemed to have swelled with fear under the jumper, but she made no sound.

He was about to break, caught in a narrow black tunnel of rage. Tina was the only other person in that tunnel. She was the only one he could hear. She had to say something.

I crouched the way she did, with my palms protecting my belly, her baby, and felt the menace of the gun. I said faintly,

"Tell him you were wrong, Tina. Tell him you don't know it's a boy. You may have said it, but you were just guessing." My voice gave out. I didn't feel like Tina, and I didn't have any faith in my advice.

She did, though, and with her sucked-in cheek barely moving next to the gun, whispered, "I was just guessing."

Geoffrey let the short nose of the gun drop a little. Without turning, he said, "Catherine?"

"Yes," I said softly, through the roar of my own fear. Even so, the word punched the air too hard and I was afraid he'd panic, but he didn't move.

"I'm sorry. I almost shot you." He sounded calm, firm, and I realized he'd made up his mind to kill Tina, maybe himself. In seconds the police would be here and things would start happening, awful things. "Where'd you get the gun?" I said quickly, trying to throw him off.

Geoffrey said, "Got it off a buddy." A short, quick laugh. Tina was crouched so low on the carpet by now that her knees were up to her shoulders and I could see the white patch of her panties. Keeping her head absolutely still, she offered me the same cool, brief smile I had seen in the kitchen that morning.

His laugh, her smile, made my fear turn black. I rose a little. I shouted at them, "Are you laughing? Laughing?" I felt like they were laughing at me, and the rage hit me so hard my eyes blurred. I stepped forward. My legs were wide, like his. Now I could almost feel his heavy combat boots on my feet. My shoulders seemed to swell and bands of anger crossed my chest behind my breasts. The force of my fury stilled the room. I took another step and said, "Don't you mess with me."

The gun wavered. "Catherine," he said, a slight shake in his voice. "You're talking crazy."

"Crazy? *You're* crazy! Both of you!"

"You've flipped, man. Really lost it."

"You bet," I shouted. I felt power in my stomach, strength in my black-sheathed thighs. I closed the space between us.

The blur passed and left a clearness I'd never imagined. I saw the edge of Geoffrey's shirt against the raw skin of his neck, the pull of blood through the veins that stood out in the hand holding the gun.

He glanced my way. "You children," I said to keep him completely unbalanced, "being tough isn't going to work here. Damn it, Tina! Do something—this isn't a game."

She crouched lower, and the tightening of her position made me reckless with exasperation. I said to her, "You've lived in my house. You've eaten my food. Now do something! Something! Tina, do it now!" I had no idea what she would do, but I felt as invincible as a boy with a gun.

She did nothing. "Tina," I screamed. "Give that baby to me!"

Now I had the rhythm, and as soon as I saw the muscles of his wrist weaken with surprise I slammed my fist down on Geoffrey's forearm and the security lady kicked behind his knees and we all sprawled with the gun spinning over the carpet to the wall, where it stopped. There was silence.

Minutes passed. Policemen filled the room and everyone began to talk. Then I felt Tina's warm breath in my ear as she whispered, "You dummy, I hated you all this time for not asking for the baby. Didn't you know?" and I looked in her clear, wet face and realized she was a child, a pregnant child, a beautiful child, mine.

The
Uncertainty
Principle

$\mathcal{A}$lice Morre was a physicist who knew from her research on computer circuitry that human beings merely imagine the real world of surfaces. Substances under extreme pressure or subject to heat or cold will flow uphill, lose force, or bond in the most unlikely unions; in general, they'll dance, twirl, or laugh in your face whenever you try to pin them down.

She was comfortable with the alien nature of things until her young husband, Olly, died suddenly of a rare infection in the heart. Then Alice found she could no longer bear the feeling that her life was a thin fiction stretched across the forces of the universe. The rabbit's foot on a key chain that Olly had given her as a joke, her tall coffee mug, the smooth stone she used as a paperweight—all the ordinary objects for which she'd had a certain fondness—now seemed threatening, foreign, unsympathetic.

At home after work, she'd sit in Olly's leather chair and look at his books and papers and wonder which ones he'd placed before he died, which ones she'd absently moved.

Daydreaming, she felt nothing, as if she'd sunk into the space between atoms. Long minutes passed.

Late one afternoon she sat in the chair eating a piece of toast, her napkin on her thigh. Periodically she scribbled stray words on graph paper to keep hold of her thoughts. She crossed her legs. The shutter slats tilted upward by themselves, blocking the California sunlight. Or at least Alice thought they did. She sat motionless in the sudden dimness. A hot breeze passed through the room. Was it a ghost?

As if coming alive, Alice stood and flipped the slats open again. She thought she saw her napkin on the floor pull itself up like a tiny tent and tiptoe over the rug. No, a napkin couldn't walk. She must have kicked it with her foot. Or maybe she'd created eddies of air current by standing to move the shutters. The napkin collapsed. Alice screamed. She snatched it up to look for the spider or whatever was behind its animation when the piece of paper in her hand folded in half. Dreading the unearthly words she was sure she'd find, Alice, with thumb and forefinger, gingerly opened the page. She spied her own fresh pencil tracks just before the paper snapped shut and dove to the floor on top of the napkin. She closed her eyes, wondering wildly if the napkin and the notepaper were going to mate.

Giggling, Alice opened her eyes and the graph paper was perfectly still, and the room was still, and her heart roared.

No, she thought, no ghost! It's me. My mind.

And then she quieted and the words came to her clearly, as if she were someone else: I wonder if I can take the pressure of living without Olly.

Alice's office in San Jose was one gray cubicle in the spread of partitions on Extel's second floor. She liked the feeling of sitting in the cross section of a beehive as she heard the small sounds of her fellow creatures at work. She put the suspect sheet of graph paper by her telephone and it lay there doing nothing, just as any sheet of bonded cellulose should.

Midmorning, Craig Ange, an engineer on her research team, brought her a chocolate doughnut, sat on the edge of the desk, and talked about his vacation in South Bimini. Craig's fresh tan made the whites of his eyes shiny. Alice noticed the sinew of his neck. She'd known him for two years and he'd checked in on her every so often since Olly's death. This morning his face seemed new, as if its contours had sharpened overnight. She touched his arm. "Thanks for sticking by me," she said.

He nodded, smiled, then grew serious. "I loved Olly too."

When he left, the word "love" shivered in Alice's mind, making her feel almost happy. Love isn't gone, just hiding, she thought, feeling irrational but strong.

She turned to her work, daring herself to unfold the piece of paper. It didn't resist. She scribbled a note, stopped for a minute, then added another idea. For three years she'd been working on a concept for stacking electrical circuits more densely so extra logic could be crammed on. The problem was heat. Movement of electrons generated tiny streams of heat that would melt circuits. Alice's mind raced with more clarity than it had in months. She filled the length of the page with her own shorthand of phrases and formulas. She was still missing one link, just one link. With a wet finger she mopped up the last of the chocolate flakes, then turned back to her notes. Where was the paper? Oh, there, crumpled in a ball at the edge of the desk. She screamed.

Craig ran in and took hold of her shoulders.

"The paper wadded up," she cried, "by itself."

Craig released his grip. Other workers crowded near, and he shooed them away. "It was you," he said carefully. "You did it."

"I didn't." She hadn't moved. Or had her mind been still, her body in motion? How would she know?

Craig picked up the ball of paper and gently pried it open.

Alice watched his hands, remembering the feel of them on her shoulders. She was scared yet relished the rush of blood to her face, the scream, as if she'd touched the pulse of a more passionate world and it made her vibrant and reckless. She gave a small smile. "No evil spirit."

"Nope," Craig said, looking at her. "No evil spirit." He pulled a pen from his shirt pocket and wrote a telephone number on the smoothed corner of the graph paper. "This is my psychiatrist," he said. "You should see him." He pressed the number into her hand. "We all miss Olly," he said. "Sometimes I catch myself dialing his extension to tell him a joke or whatever I'm thinking, and then the oddest feeling comes over me." He looked at her. "I try not to dwell on the strangeness." He paused. "I guess I'm giving you advice."

She nodded. "Somebody better."

The psychiatrist was a short, hefty man who let her choose the chair facing him instead of the couch. Contrary to her expectations, he even talked a little. Alice liked him.

"It sounds like you're having trouble accepting your husband's death," he said.

"It does," said Alice ruefully.

The therapist smiled. "Tell me about him."

She said she was so flattered when Olly asked her to marry him she didn't think of saying no. They weren't in love, being too practical for that, but he laughed at her jokes and they had a lot in common even though he designed circuits and her field was processes. Their best times were sitting in restaurants talking about work. They were colleagues and admired each other.

But soon everything besides work became grist for argument—when to make love (she preferred mornings, he nights), how to spend money (she liked to buy small luxuries, he wanted to save for big ones), and where to go for holidays (she felt it necessary to see relatives, he wanted to head for Europe). Months went by with nightly fights, and all that held them together was that they were too proud to admit defeat. Finally they each started to make compromises, and to her surprise Alice felt enriched by his perspective when she gave in to him. One evening as he walked toward her in the parking lot for their daily drive home together, she was struck by the grace of his stride. Usually they barely touched at the office, but she drew him to her in the waning sun and kissed his neck.

He smiled. "So you had a good day."

Her face against his shirt, she said, "I don't think I want to let go of you long enough to get in the car."

He lay his cheek against her hair. The final bond came unexpectedly, like the instant of crystallization.

She told the psychiatrist that she fell in love with her husband in the third year of marriage and then suddenly he was gone.

The doctor was quiet a long time. Wearily he said, "You seem to have had a healthy relationship in life. I believe you'll come to accept his death."

"No, I won't," said Alice.

When she went home, her briefcase danced, pencils dove from tables, and the shutters opened and closed at will. Alice stifled screams. She tried to keep all portable objects directly in sight, for as soon as they strayed to her peripheral vision they began to inch this way or that, dangle in midair, creep, fling themselves about, or change places with each other. "Why?" thought Alice, crossing the room to return the wet camellia to its bowl. "If I just knew why this was happening to me I could live with it." As she closed the cover on the piano keys for the second time, Olly's sheet music for "Maple Leaf Rag" jumped to the floor. Terrified, excited, Alice grabbed the music and held it aloft. The paper flapped, and then the room was still.

Alice learned to live two lives. When with people, she knew the objects would behave. Alone, she knew that nothing would stay in place for long. She learned not to scream. She slept twelve hours a day yet went to work tired and jittery. Her friends indulged her crankiness and ignored the times when she was solemn and distant. Craig asked her once how the therapy was going and she said fine. She hadn't gone back.

At all times, she hoped for an explanation. She tried to catch herself moving paper or dropping pencils. She kept a diary of her thoughts to see which ones triggered object mishaps, as she called them. The ophthalmologist who checked her peripheral vision pronounced her eyesight perfect.

That day she found the upright vacuum cleaner poised in the living room as if it had just stopped. Fiercely she pushed it over, and it clattered to her feet. "Nature abhors a vacuum," she hissed at it, then stopped, realizing what she was doing. "Goddamn it," she shouted. "I can't live like this. Let me be crazy or sane, but not both. I can't stand this."

Barefoot, she fled out the door and half ran, half walked over the successive patches of her neighbors' lawns. She crossed Lincoln Park with its small bandstand, then dashed over Foothill Expressway and ran along the bike lane. She turned east, passed a clump of houses, and entered the iron-work gate of the cemetery. She walked past granite markers for Mullen, Daggert, Mays.

Olly's stone was dark gray along the rim, lighter behind the double-edged lettering. The rectangle of new sod in front of the marker was still more vigorous than the surrounding grass.

Alice spoke to her husband. "I know you're not a ghost." She tried to calm herself, touching the bracelet Olly had given her the year before, a silver chain. The breeze, which felt empty, shifted. "I'm sure you're much too busy with cosmic things to mess up . . ." Her wavery voice scared her. She whispered, "You're not just bones either! So what's happening? Please tell me. Where are you? Olly, I've lost my place here. What can I do?"

A column of silence seemed to surround her. The light had almost completely withdrawn from the day. The summer leaves of a birch tree stood in black silhouette over the graves. Alice lay flat on the sod. All that she had ever revered—stoicism, cause and effect, being realistic about one's situation—seemed to hang suspended between birch and gravestone. Alice put her arms over her aching head as if to prevent her past beliefs from raining down on her. A leaf fell from the tree and landed near her eyelash, so close it looked blurred. She crushed it with her open hand. "Olly, I miss you!"

Then she slept. The cars whizzed past.

She awoke hours later. There were fewer cars now. Their lights flashed briefly, then disappeared. Alice sat up, brushed her hand across her cold face, and walked slowly home. As she came through the front door, a furled umbrella lifted itself out of the stand and she caught it in midair. Smiling, feeling vaudevillian, she kicked the tip, spun the umbrella in a circle, and returned it to its stand.

The next morning, Alice stood unmoving directly under the shower spray, her head gently bowed. Hot water seemed to sink into her skin. Her muscles absorbed the heat and she imagined herself a flowing liquid. She lifted her chin and let the water beat against her closed lids. Warm lights churned in the darkness of her eyes. This morning something was different. Oh yes, she'd made it to the shower without thinking of Olly. Her heart rose. She turned and opened her eyes as the wall of water hit her back.

Then she saw clearly, as if a billboard had appeared in her mind: Heat is not the enemy. She could visualize an integrated circuit and imagine its heat contained between layers. With some form of material—a new metal? a mineral?—maybe the stacks of logic could be separated; they would work together but be worlds apart.

She pushed open the glass door of the shower and wrapped a towel around herself as she hurried to her bedroom phone. Craig was still home. They talked for an hour about siphoning heat off circuits, then continued the discussion all day at work. At night, they went to Le Mouton Noir restaurant in Saratoga and walked for hours in the darkened hills.

Their conversation finally drifted to their lives, and Alice told Craig about the time she bought Olly a bike with training wheels since he'd never learned to ride. He challenged their five-year-old neighbor to a race to see who could get the little wheels off first. Craig had funny stories about Olly, too, and about his own childhood in Nome, where his father was a geologist. He said that one summer his mother bought blackout curtains and at midnight the sunshine seeping around the edges looked like slices of fire. Alice looked up at him and repeated, "Slices," and she kissed him.

A few weeks later, Alice watched Craig's face as he lay breathing beside her in her bed. A delicious sense of peace welled up in her. Soon, she thought, I'll ask him to move in with me. She imagined him saying yes, pictured making room for his books and clothes. Yes. She felt herself sinking toward unconsciousness. The instant before she joined Craig in sleep there was a slight yank on the blanket. Her mind sharpened for a second, then relaxed, and she felt the cover pull itself up and settle more snugly around Craig, tucking him in and leaving the tip of her shoulder exposed to the fresh night air.

Does Your
Tattoo Show?

$\mathcal{M}$arta and Derrin walked slowly over the blue cobble-stones, the *adoquines,* of Fortaleza Street. Marta, an experienced traveler, was empty-handed, carrying not even a purse. Her few pieces of jewelry, bought on other vacations, were locked away at home in San Francisco. She had nothing for anyone to steal. It occurred to her that she didn't even have anything to give away.

She took Derrin's arm, moving with the slightly studied grace of a tall woman. The narrow streets of Old San Juan were a maze. Glowing teenage girls swung past on stacked heels, their arms entwined with those of their lithe men. Marta thought that the tourists seemed like slow-moving blank sheets absorbing the blue of the streets and the heat and the lingering images of past armies trying to invade this Caribbean island.

Derrin and she passed a lace shop. Heat spilled down from the roofs of the shops, and she felt squeezed between the ancient buildings. She glanced at Derrin, her vacation buddy. He was balding well; his new sandals creaked. He'd been married twice. She was still married. Or was she?

The divorce papers had come in the mail three weeks earlier. With her mind empty, Marta had signed away her long-dead marriage, walked quickly back to the mailbox, and stuffed in the return envelope. She hadn't lived with her husband in years and wondered why she felt faint. She'd immediately called Derrin and left a message on his machine saying she was ready for another vacation whenever he was.

She and Derrin lived apart and told themselves they couldn't bear being tied down like other people. They'd met as consultants working on a procedures manual for a south San Francisco insurance company that later went broke. They were technical nomads and had formed the kind of tight, instant friendship that comes during late nights in basement cafeterias. At two one morning Marta told Derrin, "You know, what I've always wanted to do is travel."

"Travel?" said Derrin. "Just what I need—someone to come with me." He took her hand. "Meet your travel agent." From then on, they would head for the airport whenever they'd saved enough for another trip. Mostly they went to hot places—Cancún, Rio, even Dallas. Derrin was the most lax of travel agents. He took Marta to their destinations without reservations or plans. He could find a vacant room at the peak of the tourist season or a meal during siesta. Their train stopped abruptly once beside a rocky goat pasture in southern Italy. "Breakdown?" Marta asked anxiously, thinking of the surly residents in the last bleak town and wondering who would help them. "Doubt it," Derrin yawned. "Probably a workers' strike," and he predicted, accurately, that it would be over in an hour.

Sometimes, after Marta's trips with him, the heat would linger for a while. He would move into her narrow Russian

Hill apartment with its attic bedroom. They would set the travel alarm to watch the sunrise and swim in the numbing cold of San Francisco Bay. But gradually the abandon of the vacation would wear off. One or the other of them would get a new contract and start working killer hours. After a few days Derrin would repack his travel bag and go home to the condo in Pacifica he shared with two other guys.

The street opened to a dusty square of brown cobblestones. The fortress El Morro, which had stood firm for four hundred years, rose in the distance. Sea waves crashed against its twenty-foot-thick walls. Near El Morro's vaulted entrance was a van parked haphazardly in the dust. Black letters spelling "El Tatuaje" waved across its corrugated side. A thrill shivered across the skin of her stomach. Who would get a tattoo in a dirty van with pockmarks like bullet holes around the windows?

Marta thought of the shady street in Milwaukee where she'd grown up. She imagined her mother in the window of their brick house. Her mother would never have gotten a tattoo or even have known someone who had.

Marta thought of her mother, Rosemary, as a fragile flower. A flower grafted to a woman. She had rarely left the house. She said she had everything she needed right where she was. Her breath was light and quick, as if she were scared to use up too much oxygen. Marta was in algebra class at Estabrook High when her mother stepped off the roof and died. Maybe that was why she always pictured her mother in motion— Rosemary falling and falling.

Marta glanced around the square. She was in San Juan. Derrin beside her. The grimy van ahead.

The idea of a tattoo instantly took hold of Marta. Derrin tugged her hand but she seemed rooted in the dust. For a minute, she and Derrin stood awkwardly pulling at each other.

He could finesse any situation and she felt him looking at her, trying to find just the right joke to dispel her vacation stupor. He knew that strange cities brought eerie feelings that would disappear as soon as the town map began to make sense.

"Hey, gringo," he said, "you lost?"

She nodded, but her mind was filled with thoughts of tattoos.

Derrin dropped the smile. "You OK?"

"Yes," she said promptly, meeting his eyes as proof. He wore a pink polo shirt and chinos with creases. He had a way of rolling his clothes in a backpack so they came out wrinkle-free in the dampest climates. For the first time, she realized how carefully he avoided the bereft look of a tourist.

She hooked a finger in his belt and they started to stroll again, crossing the middle of the square. A tattoo! Ink seeping beneath her skin. Had the tattoo artist drawn those lurching letters on the side of his van? Would he scratch ink over *her* bumps and imperfections? What would she have for a tattoo? Marta imagined moist green vines spreading riotously across her flesh, their tendrils searching the curves of her hipbones, the roots twisting around her thigh. How would it feel to have a grapevine coiling her waist, or a tree climbing her calf, or a flower, a flower grafted to her ankle?

The side door of the van slid open. A middle-aged, slightly stooped man appeared, the tattoo artist. Marta gave a start. Derrin looked at her and a faint smile crossed his face.

The artist turned and watched a group of children flying kites on the grounds of the fortress. He leaned against the door with his hand clutching the roof of the van. His arm was a swirl of large-beaked birds and flying banners, but there, at his wrist, twined a single vicious flower.

How about a large heart on her back with "Mother" written inside, a sailor's tattoo? She touched Derrin's arm, but be-

fore she could speak he said, "No, you don't want a tattoo."
Though his smile was still there, Marta thought she sensed a
new gravity.

"How do you know?" Her voice sounded breathless.

"I like you just the way you are, no other decorations."

Was he vehement? Usually Derrin found a joke for everything. In Ixtapa, a two-foot chunk of ceiling fell next to her
side of the bed and Derrin woke, brushed concrete from her
pillow, said, "Now that's a bad dream," and went back to sleep.

"I need to do something," Marta said. "To celebrate my
freedom." She waited a moment. "Michel's marrying someone
he's known since childhood. I'm finally getting a divorce."
Marta wondered if she'd known anyone since childhood.
Most of her friends changed with her jobs.

Derrin said, "I didn't think you'd ever do it."

"Actually it was done a long time ago." She could hardly
remember Michel's face. She'd torn up his photos years ago.
She made herself brighten, but Derrin wasn't fooled and he
drew her to him.

"Whenever I get a divorce," he said, "I feel like a failure for
about a year."

Marta gave a little snort but felt better. "Thanks," she said.
Derrin had a knack for soothing her. The night before, she'd
wakened unsure of where she was, then had remembered—the
Ramada Inn in the tourist zone. Derrin was beside her, snoring
faintly. She followed his breathing to make herself sleep.

Now Marta lifted her chin and kissed his damp neck. "It's
not that I feel like a failure exactly," she said. "I'm not anything.
I've been careful." She put a hand on his chest. "I've kept working, kept going. But I don't know." She looked down at his
huaraches, the leather still pink like young skin. "Ten years.
What have I done? Nothing. I don't know, shouldn't I have
gone to pieces, been addicted to something, made some kind

of big mistake? Isn't that what people do who've had their hearts broken?"

Her heart felt too quiet. She'd married Michel when they were undergraduates at Berkeley. After six months he said he'd made a mistake. "I just didn't realize marriage would be so"—he searched for the word—"constant. I feel you thinking about me all the time." Marta squeezed her eyes shut. "Isn't that good?" He shrugged, "Not for me."

He moved out and joined a fraternity known for serving specialty ales at its parties. She called him every morning and left messages with his frat brothers. Then one day, she stopped trying to contact him. She didn't miss him, but now his official absence was like the swooping, weightless feeling of discovering one more step down than you'd anticipated.

Derrin was silent, studying her face. She wished he'd hug her again, but he stood with his hands at his sides. His eyes were clear, alert. He was the kind of traveler who took in details and could recount after a tour just exactly how a culture had changed. He said carefully, "With that damned Michel out of the way, you can marry me."

For a wild second Marta thought he was serious. This was her friend Derrin, who called himself a reconfirmed bachelor. What did he want? Triangular shadows crossed his eyes, making him seem hesitant. She couldn't marry him. She couldn't marry a man who spent every spare minute loping around the world, fitting chameleonlike into any society he entered. Oh, there, his face turned into full sun, erasing the questioning. Of course: a joke, part of their old lazy bantering to ease the way into a strange land. Marta smiled, relieved, feeling as if the desire for a tattoo had sharpened her life and summoned jokes that stung with a new kind of excitement. She laughed. "Well, why don't we just scare up a priest after breakfast tomorrow?"

"Good idea," he said, watching her.

The tattoo artist turned away from the kites and, looking straight at Marta, said in rounded English, "In or out?"

Her breath caught. His eyes were so black they seemed blind, yet he plied an art that didn't allow mistakes. Once laid down, the lines of his fantastic images couldn't be changed.

He clenched his fist, making the fierce flower at his wrist bloom.

Derrin pulled at her arm. "You can't be serious. Defacing your body." His eyes were back in shadow, his eyebrows bunched. Had she ever seen him angry? Before, he seemed to accept any new custom.

She was amazed at his disgust. "I need something permanent, something I can't get out of," she said.

He ducked his head. "Think about it. Needles. The ink. Please—you'll have it all your life."

All her life. Absurdly, Marta imagined her future written in a large cartoon balloon. What was she saying in it? What was she thinking? What? She smiled at Derrin, nodded.

He waved a hand at the tattoo artist—a large, American gesture. "Not today," he said. "Just looking."

Marta and Derrin sat by the window of the International Café drinking Puerto Rican coffee and eating French toast heavily dusted with powdered sugar. Marta liked the bitterness of the coffee. She knew Derrin drank it only because he wouldn't be caught dead ordering *café americano*.

Outside, two men in white shorts, no shirts, brought a wheelbarrow to the base of a hotel palm. The shorter man pulled a foot-long loop of rope from his pocket and slipped it over his bare feet. Almost magically, he climbed the palm, moving first his hands, then his trussed feet up the rough bark. He stopped, tossed a coconut to the man below. The man whacked the coconut open with an enormous machete.

"I've been thinking . . ." Marta turned to Derrin.

He looked up quickly. The hair at the sides of his head was still wet from his shower.

"I don't think I want to travel anymore," she said.

He bit a corner of crust. "I could tell."

"I didn't know myself until now."

He tapped his fork against the plate. "Why not travel?"

Marta thought he was going to say "with me" but he didn't. In the past his restraint had seemed admirable, sophisticated. Now it just seemed tight. Maybe he was the one she needed to get away from.

"I want to stay home for a while, maybe start an herb garden." Go home with a tattoo, something that would make people take notice the way she had noticed the tattoo artist. What was he doing right now? Did he live in his van? A longing pierced her. What on earth was she thinking? That she wanted a man she didn't know?

Derrin had leaned back in the wooden chair. He said softly, "How about just one more trip? I was thinking of Tahiti."

Confusion rose through Marta. She didn't know what to say.

"I like traveling with you," he continued more urgently. "You used to be so enthusiastic about everything. I liked showing you."

"You'd like showing anybody."

"Don't be a fool. I want to marry you. I wasn't kidding yesterday." The embroidered collar of his Mexican shirt lay open at the throat. He touched his fingertips to the bridge of his nose, then picked up his fork again.

Marta felt the heat of the day moving in like fever. Her voice low, she said, "You don't love me."

His chin lowered into his palm, bringing out a small wrinkle at the edge of his lower lip. He'd used tanning lotion already and his face looked baby soft. Silence. Then, carefully, "So what? We like each other. I didn't like my other wives. I've thought a lot about this."

"Not enough!" she cried. The fan above was turning, turning. The couples at the scattered tables seemed to move in slow motion, eating, looking away from each other, drinking bitterness. She said to Derrin, "How could you think that so little would be enough for me? How could you?" But then, who wouldn't, looking at her life?

He formed the crusts into a perfect square and pushed the plate away. His fingers shook. "I miscalculated."

"Badly."

They said nothing. Then he looked up from the table. "You can't deny that we have a good thing going."

She nodded. "I wouldn't want to deny it." She wondered what hours the tattoo artist kept.

Derrin took a slow breath, looked out the window. The two men had their wheelbarrow filled with coconuts. "What if I do love you?" he said. "What if I just don't know it?"

The words felt like part of the heated air. Marta couldn't quite make sense of them. She said, "If we don't hear a tree, it doesn't fall."

A long pause. Derrin put his lips together, cocked his head. "Or something like that."

She matched his half smile.

Then he sobered. "What would it take to prove I love you?"

Marta had always admired his skill at driving down a price, but now she knew how the poor women at markets felt as their profits dwindled. "You can't prove what isn't," she said. The warm air stirred. She touched Derrin's arm. He hesitated, then put his hand on hers.

Marta stood outside the van pretending to watch the squealing kids. She took a step, then back again, as if resisting a force. She felt a high singing in her head and her thoughts were jumbled.

Derrin was back at the hotel lying facedown in his red Speedo on the small rectangle of beach behind the hotel bar. She had told him she was going shopping. He had said not to hurry, he was going to take a tour of the Bacardi factory later in the afternoon.

Abruptly Marta moved forward and knocked on the van door. The sound was tinny.

The tattoo artist promptly appeared and said, "Come in." Marta followed him, feeling pulled into the darkness by a spicy smell—was it his aftershave, or a disinfectant? She couldn't speak and he didn't seem to expect her to. He perched on a high stool next to an empty one, his hands on his knees. She stood with her hand on the green vinyl seat. She was here. She said, "What about AIDS?" Too quick, too nervous.

He smiled. His young-old face was free of tattoos. Instead, concentric wrinkles eddied away from his eyes and mouth. "My needles are disposable. I'm careful. Either you trust me or you don't."

"I wish you hadn't said the last thing." Her new daring seemed to push her thoughts instantly into words.

The waves on his face deepened.

Her eyes became accustomed to the dimness. She saw a row of clear jars filled with cotton balls on the counter. Some of the balls were soaked in a yellow liquid. What looked like a handheld dentist's drill lay on a stand bolted to the floor, a foot pedal protruding from its side.

"I want one of those." She pointed to the flower on his wrist.

The body is the temple of the soul, Marta thought absurdly. Where did that come from? The Unitarian church in Milwaukee. She'd gone there for a while after her mother's death. She'd made her father take her. But the services, free-form as they were, couldn't reach her swelling emptiness.

The tattoo artist shook his head. "There's only one of these, and it's on me. Pick again."

"Are you being funny?" she asked. "Why are you smiling?"

"Not funny." He sobered. "It's hard on you. On everyone. I smile to take away my nerves." A small catch of breath. "How about a butterfly on your shoulder?"

Just like Derrin. Of course half a measure was enough for good old Marta. Was there a sign on her forehead? "No," she said, her voice too loud in the narrow space. "A serious tattoo, like that." She caught his wrist. She knew it would shock him to have her touch him. He was usually the aggressor, the one who left an imprint on the sweet and not-so-sweet.

He looked at her carefully. She saw herself in her pink pleated pants. He said slowly, "You have to be a little crazy to want a tattoo."

"Or to give one."

He blinked. "You're the kind who causes trouble later."

"I never cause trouble," she said. She still had his wrist, and he didn't pull away. "From the moment you saw me, you weren't going to give me a tattoo. You just like getting a rise out of people."

The man smiled again. He put her hand on her own chair.
"I'll give you a miniature rose on the small of your back, like
Joan Baez."

She had imagined that receiving the tattoo would be something like sex. It wasn't. She sat on the stool while the artist
taped up her T-shirt and iced her back. He worked quickly,
wordlessly. Each time the needle entered, a tiny ache bloomed
just beneath her skin. The ache grew until she could barely
stand it. Then it stopped and another ache began immediately.
Despite the pain, she got bored. She'd expected a soaring feeling. Instead she felt empty, used.

"Done," said the artist, handing her a round mirror with a
plastic handle. He held an identical mirror at her back. They
worked to get the angle right. Then she caught sight of the
angry red and blue spot circling the last bump of her spine. A
small, hurting flower grafted to her back.

"Oh," she said.

"The swelling should go down in about a week." He spoke
matter-of-factly. "You'll like it better when you get used to it.
Don't think about it now." He looked tired.

"How do you know I don't like it?"

He shrugged. "It takes people a while to know what I've
given them, as opposed to what they pictured."

Suddenly she needed to get out of that narrow, overspiced
room. "Here," she said, handing him a wad of bills in the
amount they'd agreed on. She felt awkward. The ache at the
small of her back made her uncomfortable.

"Thanks," he said. His eyelids were heavy. Would he go
home and watch TV? Probably. Marta saw in the bored circles
of his face that her dreams meant nothing to him. He'd used
them as a mild diversion for the day.

She opened the door herself and stumbled out. The blinding light almost knocked her down. Shouts. A cry. The crowd of families on the green, the kites tangling, a Frisbee slammed between father and son.

Marta walked the wide dirt path to El Morro. There was no guide and she wandered by herself from ancient pantry to dungeon to the top of the stairwell leading down, down, down to the sea. She didn't go down. Her spine seemed fragile and she thought wildly that she wouldn't be able to climb back. She must keep walking.

The adobe wall to her right dropped away abruptly to a tangle of hibiscus and she found herself outside the fortress, as if expelled. She didn't consider going back but rather walked the high street at the edge of the ocean. Low houses with sloping doors stood shoulder to shoulder. A neighborhood. Singing—or was it laughter?—wafted from a deep window.

The ache sank into Marta's innards. She sat at the edge of a grass slope and pulled her T-shirt to the side. She twisted to see the rose. No. Not possible. She couldn't see it. Her back went cold around the heat of the tattoo. He should have told her she'd never be able to see it directly. Her very own permanent decoration and she couldn't see it. How symbolic! How fantastically stupid! She pounded the grass until the tears came. You poor motherless child, she thought, you poor little girl with no place to go.

The low sun sent shadows from the houses shooting into the sea and the sound of the waves seemed to surge. Marta stood up. Her knees and ankles were stiff. She walked down the hill toward the hotel. What next? she thought, feeling dark and giddy.

Derrin was waiting for her in their hotel room, lying under the sheet, his bare, sunburned chest bent toward the book he held on his knees. "Just the person I want to see," he said. He smiled but looked wan underneath the new tan.

She sat on the bed. He was her friend. His face seemed full and open after the tattoo artist. "Sick?" she said gently and patted his stomach. She didn't love him, would never marry him, but they had something. More than most.

"Better than ever," he said. He lay down his book. *History of Polynesia.* "I have a surprise for you."

The air conditioner whirred and dripped. She didn't want any more surprises. She just wanted Derrin, the man who carried his home on his back wherever he went, like a snail.

He turned, lifted the sheet. On his bare hip, "Marta," laid over an angry red spot just like hers. She gasped. "What did you do?"

"I decided you were right. We're the kind of people who should take a plunge now and again."

"Me," she cried. "I meant me." A strange delight sang in her blood. He did this extravagant thing for her?

He took her hand and laid it on her name, which was warm. "Well, I was listening. I wanted to commemorate a once-in-a-lifetime friendship." The sunburn had caught certain angles of his body, and the soft muscles across his back seemed to ripple.

Friends, she thought.

There was a moment. Derrin took a breath. "So now you have to marry me," he said quickly. "You're free and I'm tattooed."

Oh no. Never. She looked into his face. The little crease below his lip had become permanent. When had that happened? A nerve tugged at his cheek. She had to answer. The sheet smelled faintly of mildew. Beyond the folded blackout curtains, the ocean churned.

She nodded yes. She'd tell him the truth later. He turned toward her and held her head against his chest. "I've never done anything like this before. I've been afraid. This is my first brave thing. Only brave thing. You've given me back my life."

She remembered Michel's face. The heavy, dark eyebrows, the delicate bones beneath his cheeks. Now she understood how he felt when he left her. He didn't love her. The pain he caused her was coincidental.

Marta lifted herself away from Derrin. He watched, his pale eyes wide. "I can't do this," she said.

"Don't say it." He spoke carefully. He'd anticipated her change of heart. "Not yet."

Not yet, she thought. She didn't have to make a move yet. Derrin was asking for time, the one thing she had. The sadness in the room grew until Marta could no longer bear it. Then it backed off.

Derrin moved his legs to the side of the bed, found his shorts on the floor, and pulled them on. Two stars had appeared past the salt-spattered glass.

"I got a rose at the small of my back," Marta said quietly.

He gave a short laugh. "May I see?"

He lifted her shirt gently. "Hurts like hell, doesn't it?"

She nodded. His hand on her hip was warm.

He said, "You must be tired. I had a nap as soon as I got back from mine."

"No, not tired," she said. "Yes. Exhausted."

"Here." She sat on the bed, her back against the mounded pillow. He took her bare foot in his hands and began to knead the arch as he so often did after their long walks through strange streets.

Marta pictured going home. Maybe she'd explore San Francisco as a tourist. Learn its history, its special places. "So when are you going to Tahiti?" she asked.

"Soon," he said. "Maybe next month." His warm hands seemed to mold the bones of her foot.

"I'll meet your plane when you get back."

He stopped his movements. "No one ever meets my plane," he said, his eyes shining in the last light of the day.

She handed him a pillow to lean on, thinking that someone outside the window might take them for an old couple, comforting each other. "You can tell me your adventures," she said, "and I'll tell you mine."

Chinese Tulip

I'd put off the planting too long—besides fall cleanup for the Greenspans' side yard and the Ulrichs' sprawling roses, I had five flats of tulips to put into the Hinckley garden by the end of the day. Not to mention the bed of pansies. The concrete floor of my converted garage chilled my bare feet. I leaned against my wide worktable covered now with seed trays of pansy sprouts just beginning to bloom.

It was six-thirty in the morning. With a sense of dread that had been growing for the last several months, I counted to ten and dialed Janey at the Stanford hospital. I'd promised to call every three hours. I hadn't told her the tulips weren't in the ground. She was my partner, but she had other things on her mind.

"How's it going?" I asked.

"Every seven minutes. They gave me something to calm me down, so I'm stoned." There was a moan. "Do you want to talk to Jerry while I get through this next one?"

I didn't but I said yes.

"She's doing fine," said Janey's husband. Usually I liked him, but today he seemed faintly corrupt. In a week he would be proudly telling everyone that Janey gave birth with almost no pain.

He and I made conversation while I felt the rooting soil with my finger. Early-morning California mist touched the window to my left, making me feel as if there were nothing in the world but the small capsule of me and my garage surrounded by fog. Although Janey had said she'd come back to the business when things settled down, I knew she wouldn't.

There was a fumbling on his side of the phone. Janey was back. "Oh Ruth, I wasn't going to tell you until you actually saw her, but I want to say it now . . ."

Janey had brown hair, which she frosted lightly. When she was excited she ran her fingers through her hair as if blending it all together. I knew she was doing that now, and her large green eyes would be slightly squinted as if to shield her listener from their beaming light. "Janey," I said, loving her. "You'd better tell me quick before—"

"Can't you come? How could you tell me you'd be an intruder? You're like family. You always come up with some scruple or other when no one else—oh—" She was breathless when she came back on. "We're naming her after you. Deadeye Ruth we're going to call her. How's that?"

"I like it."

She gave a groan. "I've already told her what it means—no cons, no bullshit." A grunt. "And it'll be Ruth Ann instead of just plain . . . more distinguished . . . oh my God . . . Ruth, is there something you wanted to ask me?"

Janey dropped the phone, and Jerry said good-bye and promptly hung up.

I called LaFawn Pendergast, who had answered our ad, and counted out the bulbs from the bin in the corner where Janey and I had stored them for the summer. Tulip bulbs are wonderful creatures. Their thick bases swell out in a beautiful curve that rises to a delicate point. The tuber is sheathed with the finest of skins, which is brown and somewhat shiny. Old Hinckley was getting better than he deserved.

Throwing on a windbreaker, I hurried out to my dear gray Ford truck and drove to the Palo Alto municipal dump. It smelled like the aftermath of certain dreams—vaguely unpleasant and pressing. I dragged two bags of grass out of the truck and pushed them down the wide chute. A flock of birds rose and fell delicately over the heaps.

LaFawn's powder-blue Mustang was in the driveway when I got back. She eyed me as I came toward the garage, then wandered with me among the tools and plants, unabashedly curious, as I explained the day's schedule to her. She was in her midtwenties. Her breasts rose beneath her filmy blue blouse in a broad shelf. Her belly hung over the top of her jeans. She had her pant legs stuffed into rubber, moon-man boots the same color as her Mustang.

"You said you worked in a nursery before." I patted the bulbs, my friends.

She put down a trowel. "Yeah. My ex-boyfriend was at Woolworth's Garden Center on San Antonio. He watered and lugged fertilizer."

I asked her what she did.

A moment's hesitation. "Helped him. Like I'll be helping you." She smiled. She had large gray eyes that looked out from under a green woolly hat.

We cleaned the truck and while we were loading it, I found we were almost out of bonemeal. When I got back from the wholesale supplier, it was time to call the hospital again. I wished I hadn't promised.

"Nothing's happening," said Janey through sobs. "We were going along so well, but now it's not getting any better or worse. I feel like I'm going to burst and nobody's doing anything to help me and it's just not coming. Oh Ruth, what am I going to do?"

"You're having a baby, Janey." I felt tied to a dark, inexorable process. "Your body knows what to do. It'll all be over in a few hours."

She moaned and hiccuped and then spoke more calmly. "How do you know these things when you haven't done it?"

"Believe me, I'm an expert at what I haven't done. It's the things I actually do that confuse me." Janey laughed. I imagined my entire lonely life stretching before me. "Take care," I said.

LaFawn's hat barely cleared the roof of the cab. Her legs were spread, her pudgy hands on her knees. She said nothing.

I drove slowly into the street, turned off Marsh Road with its rows of live oak, and then crossed the railroad tracks onto El Camino.

"I went to a singles party last night," LaFawn said abruptly. "In the South Bay. They had a salsa band." Her face was set deep in thought. She took off her hat and I ducked as she released a large volume of frizzy hair. "I haven't had a boyfriend in over a year. The gardener I told you about, Tommy, he said I mothered him too much. Maybe I did. Was that so bad?" She looked as though she were going to cry.

I felt squeezed into a small corner of the cab. "I think it's nice."

She leaned against the window and was silent for some time. Then she stirred. "Are you married?"

"Two years ago I was engaged. But then he fell in love with someone else. He was nice about it."

"Nice? What difference does that make? He led you right to the altar and then left?"

"It wasn't like that. We hadn't even set a date. It was very civilized. I got used to it."

"Used to it? I couldn't, not ever." She cried, first softly and then in huge sobs.

"It's all right," I said after a silence, feeling strangely comforted.

"It's not." She blew her nose.

We'd lost track of our subject but I didn't care. Her sobs had faintly steamed the windows, softening the morning light. I turned on the fan and we took Atherton Avenue, then entered the semicircular driveway of Hinckley's huge colonial with its large gray shutters and shake roof. LaFawn dabbed at her face with a fistful of blue Kleenexes, and I took one and helped her stem the flow of black mascara. I knew that Hinckley was watching through his leaded glass window.

LaFawn let out a final sigh and patted my hand. She recaptured her hair with her hat and we stepped down out of the truck.

Hinckley was on his doorstep clanking whatever it is he keeps in his pockets, brass knuckles and steely marbles perhaps. "You're late," he said.

"Now, Mr. Hinckley, let's not get off on the wrong foot. Janey's having her baby today—isn't that exciting?"

"Janey's a nice girl," he said.

He had a steady, time-eating, intrusive air. He was long retired. His right eye was filmed by a cataract, and whenever he spoke he cocked his head as if trying to peer around it.

"Hi," said LaFawn. "I'm taking Janey's place during her maternity leave." She held out her meaty hand to him.

The clanking stopped. Hinckley allowed his bent fingers to be enclosed by hers but took a step back when she showed him her pink smile. He wagged his head back and forth to see her. "Janey's a pretty good gardener," he said. He glanced at me, then back to LaFawn, giving her a skeptical look.

"She trained at Woolworth's," I said, turning to leave. Hinckley's attitude pricked me.

LaFawn shrugged. She seemed ready to cry again.

I led her through the bower with the bare wisteria vines and into Hinckley's backyard. The oval expanse of green was dotted with liquidambar trees shedding their bright red leaves.

We just didn't have time for more crying. "Put two dozen bulbs in each curve," I said to LaFawn to get her mind on business. I pointed to an area of cultivated soil on one side of the yard. Leaves fell past her face. "Tomorrow morning we're going to have to get up at the crack of dawn and put the pansies in on top. At eleven Mr. Hinckley is going to have his niece's wedding here. He wants everything to look just so."

She turned to me. "He doesn't seem like a wedding person."

"He has his favorites." I could see his pinched face through the lacy drapes in his living room window. Any minute now he'd come out and stand around sniffing. "It means a lot to him. It's the first thing he's done socially in years. We need his account."

She nodded thoughtfully, her hands stuffed into the bulging pockets of the down jacket I'd given her.

We crouched at the edge of the dirt. I held a tulip bulb up to her. "The round part goes down, the pointed part up." I quickly dug a hole with the small trowel. "You want it to be about six inches deep. Measure two fingers past the notch on the trowel." I showed her how to put in the bonemeal and she watched keenly. "Mark each one with a Popsicle stick." I handed her a bundle. "We don't want to block a bulb shoot by putting a pansy on top." As I left, she was raking furiously in a whirl of leaves.

The mowing and general cleanup of Mrs. Ulrich's yard seemed to take forever. Quickly I dug the granules of 12-12-10 fertilizer around the bases of her Montezumas. I fastened the hose to the bottle of fungicide and gave the plants a good wash. As I was wiping off the odorous, dripping bottle, Mrs. Ulrich steamed by, asking for news of Janey's baby, and then sailed back into her windowed rancher.

I called Janey from the phone booth at the Sharon Heights shopping center. She sounded weak. "Ruth, I think I'm dying. No, I don't mean it. I'm not dying, I'm just acting badly. I always thought I was a brave person but I'm not. The nurses are disgusted with me."

"Should I come?"

"You don't want to."

I thought about that for a second. "Sure I do." I could almost feel that baby shoving its way into the world.

"I don't want you to see me like this."

"Then I'll call in three hours, like I said." I was relieved.

"You always do what you say you'll do." She hung up.

I drove fast down the hill to the Greenspans' small estate. I took out the mower, filled it from the greasy gas container, and pushed it rattling across the brick belt that circles the house.

The Greenspan property was bounded by rows of bristling pyracantha bushes. I hated those bushes. Every spring, I'd sheathe myself in three flannel shirts, two pairs of jeans, and thick gloves to do battle with the tangled, spiked limbs. Sweat would sting my wounds; my hair would hang in damp, defeated strands around my ears.

Cautiously skirting the bushes, I crossed the grass feeling as if no matter which way I walked I was headed slightly uphill. I staked out a large rectangle with the mower. It occurred to me that Janey really could die. I turned the corner of the rectangle and started up the long side. A wad of grass worked its way into my sock and down to the instep of my shoe, but I didn't have time to take it out.

In two red-hot days of flu a month after my engagement broke off, I'd written out grand plans for an international mail-order tulip business. But the dreaminess of the flu had passed and now, two years later, my notes still lay folded at the back of my underwear drawer. Instead of the mail-order idea, Janey talked me into starting small with a local gardening service. I converted the garage into one big potting shed, put a file cabinet with client accounts under my kitchen desk, and we were in business. Everyone said they admired me for getting on with my life.

The rectangle got smaller and I was almost running along, muscling the mower around each turn. Mashed green stalks flew into the air and as I left the finished heart of the rectangle, I almost whirred right into the pyracantha lurking at the corner of the Greenspans' back deck.

There was a yellow-gray film over the sun as I got out in Hinckley's driveway. LaFawn was sitting on his doorstep, her hair a cumulus cloud sailing past her eyebrows. Her face was shiny and flushed. The door behind her was open and I could hear Hinckley, his thin voice hoarse, arguing with a woman inside. LaFawn stood up but I pushed past her.

The woman was young and wore small pearl drops on gold earrings that sparkled. She and Hinckley looked at me, the force of their argument still frozen on their faces.

I grabbed the phone that was in a recessed space in the hall. "Jerry, is she all right? I had a premonition and—"

"Your premonition was right."

I gasped.

"We have a beautiful baby girl, eight pounds, ten ounces, and the doctor says she's never seen a healthier child. Janey can't talk just now—they're in with her—but she's fine and she's so happy. Ruth, you've been her faithful friend. I'm so tired . . ." His voice trailed off.

I hung up with a trembling hand and rushed past Hinckley and his niece, who were now so deep in their argument that they didn't notice me at all.

LaFawn and I reloaded the camper with the empty bulb boxes and the tools. The haze over the sun had thickened.

"Next spring, oh, I can't wait to see those bulbs come up," she said as we climbed into the truck. "I feel great—better than I have in a while. I feel useful."

We pulled into the street. She looked at me, then reduced herself to fit into my mood. She followed the cross scents of human interaction with a fineness I had forgotten possible. I had been like that once.

"What happened?" she asked finally.

"Janey had her baby and everything is just fine."

"The baby. That's wonderful."

I just wanted to get home. I felt as though sticky green glue held my parts together. We rode home without talking until I asked LaFawn to come at five the next morning. She said that would be all right.

I bathed and plunged into bed and slept like I'd sunk to the bottom of the ocean. The phone blasted me out at nine. It was black outside. Janey's voice was lyrical. "Ruth, she's so ugly it's terrifying. She's beautiful. Please, please come see us now. I'm not tired and I need to talk."

The sleep was heavy in my throat. "I can't come tonight."

Silence on the line. "Why not?"

"I don't know. I just can't."

She spoke to me, then her voice stopped, and I was asleep as soon as the receiver clicked.

There was a pounding at the door like a summons. I looked at the snooze alarm clock. Two-fifteen in the morning. The thumping went on. I got up.

LaFawn tumbled in the door, breathless, her cheeks enflamed. Her hair stuck out of her cowboy hat as if it had grown rapidly. She had my down jacket pulled over her nightgown. Blue ruffles fell around her neck and stuck out from the jacket at her wrists.

"What on earth is it? Are you hurt?" I led her into the living room.

"No, not me." She collapsed on my couch in a series of sighs.

"If no one's hurt, anything else can be fixed."

She pulled off her hat. "You don't understand. Mr. Hinckley's wedding. I put all the bulbs in too deep. I remembered it was two fingers, but I measured past the whole trowel, not just the notch. As soon as I got home, it hit me. I was going to tell you in the morning but I couldn't sleep." Her eyes began to water. "I haven't done anything right in a long time and I started out so well. Look how fat I am." She patted her belly. "How did that happen? I just like to eat and now I'll never have a boyfriend again."

Now that she had on no makeup, her dark eyebrows stood out. They moved subtly with each expression and I wondered at the fine muscles we all have. She sat up. "Well," she said, letting out a large wash of air. "You don't seem too upset." She looked at me carefully.

"Upset?" I put on a mock pout. "Just think, even now those bulbs are sinking down into the center of the earth. They're getting lost. And it's all your fault."

She gave me a half smile. "I've never met anyone like you before." She spread one hand on the couch. "You don't care about anything."

My fingers were cold, the tips especially. "That's not yours to say."

She looked down.

We sat quietly for a long time. I wondered where I could go from here. "Mr. Hinckley is just an old crock," I said. "We can leave them that way. Some of them will make it up. The rest he'll never notice."

"Yes, he will." She put her hand to her cheek. "He notices everything. And he'll know I screwed up."

"Or we can just tell him the pansies can't go in until next week," I said. "After we have a chance to make some, ah, adjustments."

Her eyebrows followed my every word. "But what about the wedding?"

"What difference are a few pansies going to make?"

Her eyebrows drew tightly together, with one raising slightly every once in a while. Her shoulders sagged. The jacket hung open and I could see her body sloping downward inside it. As each minute passed, she seemed to be drooping closer to the ground.

I got up. "C'mon, we can do it tonight. No one will be the wiser."

LaFawn's look was cautious but she moved to rise from the couch.

"Hurry up, we have barely enough time."

The rain began just as we were getting out of the truck. We crouched along Hinckley's driveway and I thought of him alone in his bed, his spare body dry, his breath shallow.

The liquidambars rustled in the wind that was growing ever stronger. Leaves fell on our shoulders.

With the garden shears, LaFawn cut lengths of the yellow rope I'd brought, then rigged a blanket between a shovel and the prong on the fence closest to the house. With the blanket at her back, LaFawn shone my large red flashlight on the garden soil, illuminating the Popsicle sticks standing guard over the buried bulbs. I stood behind her to see if any light leaked out and it did a little, but not enough to awaken Hinckley.

I set furiously to work in the wet soil, digging out the first bulb from its deep niche and reburying it nearer the surface. I had 239 left to go.

Kneeling, I plunged myself into the soil, seeking each precious cone and replacing it in a closer incubation. After righting a cluster of bulbs, I scooped six pansies out of their soil squares and planted them in rows above.

The wind heightened steadily as if it were required to reach a certain velocity by an appointed time.

LaFawn was a wonder. She kept the flashlight trained firmly on each Popsicle stick in turn. As we moved along the fence and established a routine, she managed to have a pansy waiting for me each time I needed one, its roots gasping in the sudden open. All along, she was able to keep the light from reaching Hinckley, supply me with plants, indicate where I'd missed a stick, and retrieve the blanket when the wet wind caught a flapping corner of it.

One minute it was darker than it had ever been, and the next you could see the first speck of light spread out over the whole curve of the sky, one drop of white stretched impossibly thin. The rain became a sheet of mist that clung to our hands and faces like another, better skin.

I tamped the last pansy in as LaFawn turned off the flashlight. The edges of her muddy nightgown hung before me. I looked up at her. She was smiling. She took off her hat and put it on my head.

We gathered the pile of Popsicle sticks and the gray plastic sprout pans scattered on the wet grass. Hinckley came out of the house. He was in a striped bathrobe that stopped at his knees. His face was even paler and more lined than usual and the tuft of gray at his throat looked as if it might crumble.

"Good morning," I said, feeling fine.

He nodded at me and then I saw that he'd been crying.

"We got the pansies in," said LaFawn, taking a step toward him. "We did it early so you wouldn't worry."

"It doesn't matter." His skin was so pale it was almost blue.

LaFawn, pink and round by contrast, would have nothing to do with this attitude. "It's good to have it done early for—your—party." She began to speak more distinctly, as if it occurred to her that he might be deaf. "You—need—to—have—extra—time—to—iron—out—any—last-minute—details."

"There's not going to be a wedding." He put a veined hand to his forehead. "My niece called it off. She said I was impossible. She said they were going to City Hall in San Francisco and then they'll take their friends to Julius Castle restaurant and that'll be it. She said I might as well know they've been living together for four years anyway."

LaFawn took a step back, pulled the jacket around her. Drops of mist gathered on the pansies, weighed the leaves down, and then slid off.

Seeing LaFawn's stricken face seemed to rejuvenate Hinckley. He put his hands in the patch pockets of his robe. "Well," he said, "you'd better come in. You're soaked and I don't want you suing me for pneumonia."

He led us inside and made us stand on newspapers in the small room next to the telephone alcove. I took off my tennis shoes and Hinckley slipped out of his cracked slippers. We lined up our footwear on the pages of newsprint. Hinckley brought towels and we all dried our feet and put on the thin, ribbed socks that he insisted we wear.

We three padded into the living room, where I had never been before. It was filled with heavy mahogany furniture. On an end table lay a white guest book with gold trim. A black upright piano stood opposite the slate fireplace.

"Nice piano," said LaFawn, running her hand along the keys.

"Thanks," said Hinckley. "I bought it for my niece in hopes she would learn to play." He sat on the long, skirted couch looking dazed.

Finally he asked us if we would like a drink to warm us up and shuffled out, returning with a magnum of champagne, which he explained was to have been a present for the best man. "We should drink a toast," said LaFawn as Hinckley popped the cork.

He and I looked at her with irritation.

"All right, we'll just drink," she said.

So we drank wedding champagne all that morning as the mist turned to rain and then back to mist. Mr. Hinckley played "Pennies from Heaven," then taught LaFawn and me the lyrics. We sang each verse three times.

I looked out the rain-spotted windows at the garden and thought what a beautiful blurry sight it was.

At noon, I put my empty glass on top of the piano. I took a breath and said that one day when we were sober I wanted to discuss a business proposition with them. But just now there was someone I had to visit. I told them about my namesake.

We walked into the garden. Red leaves drifted by. Then I noticed that we'd missed one—a Popsicle stick was still standing in the second curve of the fence. Just the right way to begin, I thought, imagining myself taking Ruth Ann in my arms. I would tell her the tale of the two gardeners who planted a tulip so deep it turned right around and grew straight to China.

You Can See
Jupiter with the Naked
Eye If You Know
Where to Look

*M*y brother, Steve, was short, which he hated, so he said he was taller than I was and he almost convinced me. In 1962, when he was twelve and I was ten, I could look down on his head and see the white scalp through the short bristles. He took great pains to get his hair to stand up straight and asked me if I thought it looked good. I was amazed that my opinion mattered to him.

That was the year he began to call me by my full name, Eleanor, which no one else did. When the telescope he had ordered through the mail came after endless weeks, he let me slit the tape around the large oblong box addressed to Mr. Stephen Bates. The next day, he cut off the eyelashes of his right eye to see through the thing better and Mother said in her vague, slightly critical voice that the world doesn't make it easy for extremists. A red blotch spilled out on his neck, as it did whenever he was angry or excited. "The world doesn't make it easy, period," he responded. She leaned back on the daybed, a bewildered woman who spent most of her time in the guest room reading.

I think of my mother as long, not tall, lying with *Mrs. Dalloway* in her hand, a blue blanket over her knees, and her awkward, imposing feet placed side by side as if unsure of their task. Steve told me once that he figured out he was born five months after she and Father were married.

Steve went to the Graham Funt School for gifted children in Palo Alto. His teachers said he could expect great success in life. He had many projects. Mother said he would probably squander his genius by flitting from one thing to another. I told her that wasn't fair—no one knew what the future would bring. She adjusted the blanket. "True," she said.

The week after Steve got his telescope, our neighbor Cyril Stanton, a small, sour widower with a dog that yapped at every passing breeze, broke ground for a bomb shelter in his front yard. Mother was furious at the stupidity and unsightliness of it; Steve was intrigued. For days, he spent every spare moment next door talking rads and concrete thicknesses with Stanton.

After a dinner of PromptPizza takeout at the kitchen table one evening, Father and I heard Steve arguing with Mother in the guest room, which she had retired to. Steve told her he was going to be a lawyer. She said good luck. He asked her what she meant by that. She turned a page—we heard it crinkle. "I just mean that lawyers need stick-to-itiveness," she said.

"Oh, I suppose that's why you never went back to school."

Father and I looked at each other. I bent my last piece of dough and put it back in the pink cardboard box. He folded his hands under his chin. He had a round, apologetic face that was always shiny, as if someone polished it for him.

There was a silence. Then Steve emerged looking as if he had been crying. He said he was going out. I said I'd go with him, but he took his telescope and left alone.

The next morning, he found me in the backyard dumping the remains of the pizza in the dented metal garbage can. I was relieved to see him restored after the argument. He told me we were going to bike to the hills behind Stanford. The excitement of his adventurous life spilled over me and I was proud to be his associate. But it wouldn't do to lose my dignity. "What about Mr. Stanton? I thought the cement truck was coming today."

"I'm finished with that." The blotch stood out again. "I want to show you something else," he said.

I tore into the kitchen to make sandwiches. On the brick-patterned linoleum floor of the kitchen was a newspaper spread wide and, on it, a brown shoe-polish can with a rag. Father, who was a real estate agent with Hare, Brewer, and Kelley, must have left early to show some clients a house. He had said one night at dinner that if interest rates fell to $3\frac{3}{4}$ percent an era of prosperity was bound to come. Mother was not at the table to refute him. It was my understanding that being a real estate agent was some kind of failure. I put the rag and polish under the sink.

Mother hadn't been in a cooking phase for some time, so it was hard to tell what I might find in the fridge. I found two eggs with black Xs on their shells, peeled them, and made tuna and chopped-egg sandwiches, Steve's favorite. I wrapped them in waxed paper—Mother said sandwich bags were wasteful. I wrote a note telling her where we were going and put it under a plastic watermelon magnet on the fridge. The kitchen was still. I tried to leave quietly so as not to awaken her, but she called out from the bedroom, "Be careful, Elly."

I turned. "I will."

Steve and I emerged from the garage blinking in the summer sunshine. The morning fog was burning off but there was still a fuzziness around the sun. The grass gleamed. Stanton's dog barked and whined. I threw the kickstand up on my blue Schwinn and pedaled furiously away.

I heard Steve seize his English racer. Soon he floated by, his face white and happy.

Oh yes, I said to myself, not knowing what I meant. I was strong and courageous. I leaned into a turn and felt my body right the balance. I had a fleeting thought of riding my mother on the handlebars, showing her the morning.

Steve slowed and waited for me and we continued side by side. The wind bent his hair back. He held the handle grips tightly, his knuckles white, so that his bike seemed propelled not by the pedals but by the energy his hands squeezed down through the steel frame and into the wheels.

The homes became larger, the lawns deeper, with curved pathways. We turned off Sandhill Road and walked the bikes to the Stanford golf course. We propped the bicycles against a eucalyptus tree. They leaned together as if whispering of bike things—hot asphalt, curbs, and treacherous grates.

My brother lifted the bottom of the wire fence for me as I ducked under. Then I did the same for him. "We shouldn't be here," I said. With the wire at my back, I felt trapped. "There are reasons for fences, you know."

"It's all right. Mom went to school at Stanford. Anyway, the course is closed on Mondays. No one will know."

I remembered only vaguely that Mother had ever done anything other than read all day. Steve and I walked across the deep green grass. It smelled freshly cut.

"Mr. Stanton sent for twenty cartons of dried Stroganoff mix to store in his bomb shelter," Steve told me. "He said that if anyone tries to get in the shelter he'll shoot to kill."

"Shoot to kill?" I asked. "Does that mean us?"

We followed a cart path to a stand of willows. "I suppose so," said Steve.

In my inner ear I could hear the whine of the sirens and feel the cold sweat of the last few moments on earth.

"You wouldn't want to live in a world that had been hit by a nuclear bomb," he said, squinting.

That's what he didn't know. I would. Oh yes I would. I turned my face away. I wouldn't tell even him what I would do with those last precious moments before the world ended. My brother and the rest of them would turn their faces to the sky, cross their arms over their chests, and whistle a tune as they waited for the huge gray cylinders to speed toward them. Not me, not me. I would shoot to kill, like our crabby neighbor.

I peeked at my brother. He was walking with his head down, his jaw set. The blotch on his neck had faded but for a reddish border below his earlobe. No, I would never tell him that his sister was a terrible outlaw, a kicker, a scratcher, greedy and mean.

As we walked, the heat grew. "Do you want to sing?" Steve asked, looking up the hill.

"No, I don't want to sing." I rarely crossed him, but just then I could not do what he wanted.

He rubbed his neck. A lone, furtive golfer whacked at a ball in the distance. "I saw Jupiter last night," Steve said. His mind jumped from one thing to the next.

"I didn't think you could see Jupiter. It's a planet. It doesn't give off any light." I wanted my brother to know that I learned some impressive facts even at my ordinary public school.

His face was strange and exultant. "Where'd you get that idea? There's plenty of light in the universe to see Jupiter. In fact, it's one of the naked-eye planets. You could see it yourself if you knew where to look."

A single cloud took a chip out of the sun. I shrugged. Through the trees we glimpsed the red roofs of Stanford's classrooms and libraries. Steve pointed at them. "Did you know there's a Russian revolutionary in their library? He studies there."

"A revolutionary? Like Nathan Hale?" I was studying the American Revolution. Steve had told me once that minor heroes were sometimes more interesting than major ones, and I wanted him to see I'd taken him to heart.

His face glistened in the sun. He'd hardly heard me.

I imagined him as a revolutionary. He would write pamphlets and spy on the enemy in disguise. Would he get caught? I could see him standing on the scaffold, his hands bound behind his back. He'd shout down to me that he wished he had another life to lose for his country. I wanted to tell him to change his ways now, before he got into serious trouble.

"What's a Russian revolutionary doing in California?" I said instead.

Steve faced me. "He's a White Russian named Alexander Kerensky. He was in power for three months in 1917. Then he got thrown out too. No one would listen to him." He paused. "There's a lot going on that we don't know about. Out there . . ." He swept his hand across the sky.

"You talk too much about scary things," I said.

He wiped his face with his shirt. "Someone has to talk about them."

I was tired from the long bike ride so instead of continuing up into the hills, which was what Steve wanted to do, we stopped for lunch at the narrow beginning of the San Francisquito Creek. The shallow water moved slowly, bulged toward us, then rambled on over a bed of pebbles.

"Look at them," I cried, running down the weedy bank and crouching on a log at water's edge. "Millions of them." Small dark bodies of pollywogs slithered through the water. Some were still fish; some had legs and a tail and the beginnings of eyes. Others had no legs at all and swam rudderless, unaware of their fate. "Let's take them home."

Steve sauntered down the bank and stood with his hands in his pockets.

I stood up. The tadpoles seemed insignificant compared to his own mysterious projects. I wiped my wet hand on my jeans. I was too old for frogs but I persisted. "We can drink the pop and then put them in the bottles."

He slipped the day pack off slowly but I noticed he guzzled his bottle of Orange Crush as fast as I did mine. The bubbles seemed large in my throat. I waded into the stream and began slipping the tiny creatures headfirst into the bottle from my cupped hand. Their gray-green bodies were soft. I loved the feel of them squirming in my hands.

"You've got too many," said my brother, grabbing my hand and tilting the bottle over the stream to let three flop out.

"What's too many?" I cried, pulling back from him. He and my mother always had regulations.

"If the population is too dense they get sick," said Steve.

"I'll put them in jars when we get home."

"Why do you want them?" He stood on a rock.

"I just do." I trapped more of the velvet bodies with my hands. Steve shrugged.

We put our bottles on a rock in the shade and Steve got two red bandannas from the pack. He spread them on the grass at the lip of the bank for us to sit on. I took out the sandwiches.

The food gave me a luxurious feeling and I stretched out on one elbow. Below us, a tadpole with legs fore and aft came to the edge of the glass, then sank. My mind turned to other things. More easily now, I thought again about the sirens. I imagined Steve and me as the only survivors, building a house out of the rubble. A real house, not a bomb shelter. With dirt maybe or the red tiles from Stanford's roofs.

The roar of the motorcycles seemed to loom out of the trees. I pinched Steve and he looked up from his own reverie. Two teenage boys, one on a heavy black Honda, the other on a cycle with bulging saddlebags in back, were coming at us along the cart path. We stayed still on our small mound of tall grass. I could barely see the boys' faces as they roared toward us, but I could smell the Brylcreem and beer mixed with the odor of the exhaust.

When they were about fifty feet away, the boys wheeled the bikes and faced us. Then, laughing, they started for us again. One had long hair slicked back and a large jutting chin. The other was skinny and very pale. They yelled obscenities.

I was on my feet. "Don't you say that!" I screamed above the engines.

The skinny one gunned his machine but stopped for a moment, and I could see the bristles of his sideburns. "We're the Stanford patrol," he said, still laughing. "You're trespassing."

The other boy kept coming slowly along the path. I stood my ground until I could see the chain across the top of his boot. A rock was hurled against me as if dropped from heaven. My brother and I rolled down the bank unhurt.

The bikers roared off, yelling to each other.

Steve sat up. A weed with a tiny yellow star flower lay lightly on his shoulder. "Are you all right?" he asked, crawling over to me.

My right temple was numb; my hands burned. I nodded.

He grabbed my elbow. "Don't ever fight with someone like that," he said. "It doesn't do any good." Blood oozed from a scratch on his chin.

"They shouldn't run us down." I put my hands together. "Who's trespassing? I'm sure the golfers want tire marks all over their course."

"Forget it!" he said, grabbing my shoulders. "You don't understand."

"No, I don't. We have to stand up for ourselves."

"If I hadn't pushed you down the bank you could have been killed." His breath was hot in my face.

I turned away, realizing he was the one who had saved me. There was silence but for the rustle of the trees. The motorcyclists were not coming back. "I hope they didn't trample our lunch," I said, "I still had half a sandwich." I wanted to make him laugh.

He did and we climbed back up the bank.

After eating, we lay on our backs and napped for a couple of minutes. There were no clouds at all.

Steve spoke. "Mom was going to be a lawyer," he said.

I removed a pebble from beneath my shoulder bone. I couldn't picture it. Being a lawyer seemed like the kind of thing only Steve could do. In fact, I felt a little resentful that she'd intruded.

He sat up. "Actually, instead of being a lawyer, I've decided to be a judge. I think we need people like me to be judges—people who see both sides." He folded the waxed paper.

A judge. Yes, that would suit him. I could picture him pounding with his gavel and demanding silence in the name of justice. The criminals would thank him for his fairness even as they clanked off to prison. "You would have to sit all day," I said. "You wouldn't like that."

"I'd be older then."

"You'd have to wear a wig!"

He gave a snort of approval.

Contentment eased over me. We decided to leave the tadpoles and get them later. They were peaceful floating one on top of the other.

We continued across the golf course and through the fence into the hilly cow pasture that Steve said was Stanford land too. The path upward was rutted and I walked on one side, Steve on the other, in the direction that had pulled at his attention all day. His face was pale again.

Now I would have enjoyed singing but we walked in silence. I had learned from my mother and my brother that it was a cardinal sin to break someone's concentration. We climbed for so long that my knees ached.

Finally the path flattened out for about a hundred yards. As we approached the last swell of land, Steve stopped as if struck. "There," he breathed, not looking at me. "I found it last night when I was hunting for a place to put the telescope."

Ahead of us on the next hill was a huge disk, like an antenna, as tall as a five-story building. Its steel lattice was painted white. It had two struts advancing from either side that joined in the middle, forming a giant triangle. The updraft breeze rattled through the crisscrossing frame holding up the face of the antenna. It sounded like a thousand almost muffled wind chimes.

My hands turned cold. My forgotten fears came back redoubled—some of the marks on the ground were the tire treads of motorcycles. "We shouldn't be here."

"It's all right," my brother said, entranced by the disk. "Let's go look in the trailer at the back."

"I don't think we should."

But Steve walked right up to the trailer and held his hands around his face to cut the glare of the window. He motioned to me to look in also. It was an office. On the desk was a stack of light blue papers. A dark blue line peaked and dipped across the large piece of graph paper tacked on the wall. On the table was a coffee cup with a monkey face on it.

"Maybe those greasers were connected with this," I said breathlessly, thinking of the spinning spokes. We walked to the front of the disk again. It towered over us.

"No, of course not," Steve said, standing with his back to the antenna, his face turned up to the sky in the same attitude, as if communicating with a distant correspondent. "It's more important than any thugs."

The wind in the dish had become eerily beautiful. I felt as if I alone had escaped the antenna's special powers. "So what do you think it is?" I asked him. "Tell me. I know you have an idea."

Steve spread his arms and I almost expected him to fly. He had waited all day for this moment.

"I think it's a new way for our intellectuals to talk to their intellectuals. I think Kerensky is here to help with the translation and teach us about the Russians so that we can understand each other better. I think it's a way to prevent war." He stood on his tiptoes and then rocked on his heels and looked back up at the dish again.

The red roofs of Stanford glowed far below, and across the bay blue-gray hills faded to nothingness. A sense of distance came over me as I felt my brother's longing to find, and talk to, the enemy, to know everything simply and easily. I wanted to fly down the weedy slope on my bike. I wanted to tell Kerensky to leave California, to take his awful ideas, whatever they were, and quit stirring my brother up.

"It's amazing, isn't it?" Steve asked softly.

I said we had better get the tadpoles and turned my back on that horrifying antenna.

The tadpoles were smashed against the rocks, their dead eyes still open, their little guts spilling out on the earth against slivers of glass. Dead, they looked even more numerous than they had alive. The smell of exhaust was in the air. I began to cry.

My brother was stricken. "The creeps! The creeps!" he shouted. "The dirty, goddamned creeps." He scraped up one of the bodies and threw it into the stream. "Christ almighty, can't they leave anything alone?"

"Let's call the police," I said.

"It's no use. Police don't care about frogs." He tossed another one in the creek. He was shaking. "It's all your fault," he hissed at me. "You wanted them."

The blood thudded in my ears. Was it my fault?

A tadpole lying in the dirt twitched its tail and Steve stepped on it viciously. The deed seemed to fuel him and he took a large shard and shattered it against a rock, then stamped on another wounded tadpole wriggling desperately toward the water.

"Don't," I shouted at him. "Don't do it. You're right—it's all my fault." Every word intensified the blotch on his neck.

He seized the broken bottom of one of the bottles.

"Don't hurt any more of them!" I screamed, snatching at the glass.

He grabbed my hand. I pulled away as hard as I could but he held my wrist and brought the jagged glass down onto my arm, just below my elbow. He held it there, but lightly, and when he let me go and I stumbled backward, there was no blood. My brother looked at me, his nostrils wide, his chest heaving. He let out a long, singing, sorry wail and then he bent his head and cried.

The radio dish quickly became obsolete. It had been built by the navy to study the feasibility of using the moon to return radio waves. Interest rates soared but real estate values rose even faster. My father sold condominiums and became a millionaire; my mother quit getting out of bed altogether. The cold war ended. My brother grew tall and became a poet. I am the judge.

Lifetime
Achievement

*H*aving his father and mother make their quiet move to The Cascades, a retirement community, wasn't the dramatic development Grant Snyder had expected. He had always imagined one final, large-screen battle with his father—a Cecil B. DeMille spectacle with wheeling horses and cries of anguish. Now he felt cheated.

Grant and his father, Eugene, faced each other across the workbench in the basement of Grant's childhood home. Humming a little to himself, Eugene laid out the tools in processionary order. He seemed to glow with the special glee he reserved for the befuddlement of his only son. He stopped the breathy tune. "Sell them or keep them yourself," he said. "I've worked out the prices if you sell." He patted a skill saw.

The overhead light fixture swayed from its cord as if Eugene's mere presence caused the room to rock. Grant looked at his father in the moving light. He was surprised, frightened to see such a well-used face around those pale eyes. "They're just old tools," Grant said. "Who would want them at any price?"

Feeling foolish over his ill humor, Grant put his hands in the pockets of his jeans. He had driven the twenty-two hours to Seattle from UCLA with a stack of sixty ungraded Film Criticism exams beside him. He was worn out. He thought he was the one who became more tired and anxious the older his father got. And this great retirement farce wasn't helping.

The joke was that Eugene Snyder had never really worked. His brothers had paid him to stay away from the family bank. He spent his life creating occasions, such as this one, then laughing when others got caught up in the solemnity of the moment. His son, Grant, was his chief target.

As if cued by Grant's thoughts, Eugene lovingly raised a pipe wrench. He exaggerated the gesture so that Grant was aware of each square fingertip on the metal. His father was playing the part with the pathos of a fine, aged actor in his last role.

"Sears backs this with a lifetime guarantee," said Eugene to his son. The white and black hairs of his eyebrows curved down toward wily eyes. "That should add some value." A look of sadness. "Wouldn't one of your students want them?"

"My students think something like a toilet is a symbol. They wouldn't know how to repair one."

His father forced a smile and allowed his sorrow to lift by a degree. He stacked squares of sandpaper that he had pulled out from the bottom of his toolbox.

"You know, Dad . . ." Grant felt odd saying "Dad." "I expected you to live in this house for years. I pictured myself coming home on holidays and fixing the plumbing and things."

From the time Grant was in high school he had been the one to take care of the tall Victorian facing Elliott Bay. His father was no good with his hands, and Grant had enjoyed the work—the setbacks when joints wouldn't give or wires couldn't be traced and then the victories of dripless gaskets and new fixtures that snapped on.

"You thought Mama and I would rattle around in this old house until you came in and picked up the pieces." Eugene smiled. There were cracks at the corners of his lips, as if his mouth had folded under the weight of his repertoire of expressions.

"Something like that." Grant rested his palms on the bench. "They play bridge at those places." He was reacting to his father's act, as he always did. The muscles tightened in Grant's stomach. He wondered if his father would have been able to develop his eccentricities so finely if he didn't have such a foil for a son.

A smile with cheeks but not eyes. "I can learn," said Eugene.

"You've always disliked the kinds of people who play bridge," said Grant. "Anal retentive, you called them." Did his father really plan to perform now for a bunch of old people, even stylish old people who played tennis and cruised to the Bahamas?

"Did I?" Eugene began putting the tools back in the long box. Each had a place.

"Yes, you said that." Grant came around to his father's side of the bench. "And you told me you loathe condominiums because they're designed by the same architects who do cell blocks. I'm using your words. You have an aversion to a low-salt diet. They have a special low-sodium dinner every other day. The director told me yesterday when I called to see what you'd gotten yourself into."

"Don't you think your mother deserves a rest? She won't have to cook anymore."

"Don't do this to me, Dad."

"Do what?"

"All of a sudden do this incredibly sensible thing. I'm not prepared for it." Grant smiled though his face felt stiff. His friends' parents were off on strange treks, buying motorcycles and breaking their necks in Nepal. Those were the kinds of things Grant's father had done when he was younger, when all the other fathers were earning a living. "Peter Coover's parents spent their savings on a sailboat."

"I don't like sailing," said Eugene.

"Well, now they don't have a dime and live in this boat in a friend's backyard." Grant laughed. "It's pitiful."

His father gave a slow-spreading grin that would have made a nice tight camera shot. He chuckled.

"Why can't you be pathetic when you should?" said Grant. The sway of the light made him dizzy.

"You think I was pitiful too early?"

The truth of it shot through Grant's stomach. He tried not to change demeanor, but Eugene always knew when he had won. "Just a little," said Grant, keeping the smile frozen on his face.

"Just a little pitiful," said his father. "It sounds like a song." He reached up and stopped the swinging green cone of the lamp, then snapped off the light. For a moment, father and son stood in the darkness. Grant could hear only his father's whistling breath. He willed himself not to speak or move. Finally Eugene turned the light back on again. "Oh, are we still here?" he said, laughing. The bluish circles intensified the glow of his eyes.

"For the moment," replied Grant as the tears welled and he pictured burying his father with all these tools, like a pharaoh entombed with his belongings. Grant thought of his father waking up at the last minute screaming and gasping and imagined that he was the one appointed to pat him back into the earth.

Grant's mother gave him a tour of their condo while Eugene signed up for a tennis lesson. The place seemed too small and too bright. His mother sat on the undersized sofa and spread paint samples on the glass table before them. "Cool colors make a room look bigger, don't you think?" she said.

He nodded. His mother's reading glasses had slipped on her nose and she looked cockeyed and beautiful. Grant thought extravagantly that she burned more brightly the wilder his father got.

"Your father takes care of me in his own way," she said.

"Does he? Whose idea is this?" Through the years, his mother had talked herself into many things to love her strange husband.

"Your father has ideas far ahead of me. I have faith and you should too."

"In a crazy man? I was just thinking this morning about the time he painted red footprints around the opera house at the Seattle Center."

His mother delicately leaned an elbow on one of the cushions. She had one smile only and it filled the room. "I pulled you out of study hall to bail him out of jail."

"Do you know what I endured at school?" Grant leaned forward and his knee hit the table. "My friends were protesting Cambodia and my father was boycotting a tenor."

"We each play our part." She could tease too.

"I told him I died of embarrassment every day. I was seventeen years old. Do you know what he said?"

"Let me guess." She folded her hands together.

"He said we all have to die of something."

"And you call him crazy?"

Eugene came back and asked what was so funny and insisted his son stay for dinner.

Grant picked at the tasteless chicken cacciatore and watched his mother as his father talked. In public his parents paid attention to each other with zealous admiration.

A few of the residents at the other tables were in wheelchairs, but most looked fit and tanned. The men wore suits, the women good cotton dresses with pastel cardigans. Grant felt shabby, overweight, and too young. He was afraid that if he spoke his voice would come out high and awkward.

Eugene began talking politics. His voice boomed and the diners at the three nearest tables had to listen to avoid appearing rude. A gentleman with white hair combed straight across the top of his forehead smiled at Eugene, his fork suspended in midair. Eugene told him they all should vote for the dead sheriff of King County. The man blinked.

"What happens if he wins?" asked his companion. She adjusted the pearls at her throat. The man twinkled at her, then chewed with studied thoughtfulness.

"It will invalidate the election," said Grant's father. He waved his hand for emphasis and his sleeve brushed through his ice water. Grant moved the glass.

He watched his father out of the corner of his eye. There was fear in the bunching of the wide eyebrows, the thinness of the lips. Grant wondered why Eugene couldn't just lay low for a while, wait for acceptance. But that wasn't his father's way.

"The opponent—" thundered his father.

"The live one?" mocked the woman with the pearls. She flashed straight, capped teeth. Grant considered dropping into his plate—Alex DeLarge in *A Clockwork Orange*.

"The live one," said Grant's father, "is—ha!—a live one!" He looked around at the other tables. "Hear that? A live one!"

"I think I'm ready for dessert," said Grant's mother. Her shoulders were narrow, her back straight. She became more erect the more effort she put into pretending that her husband was being charming. Grant gave her a supportive smile but she didn't see or pretended she didn't.

"Seriously," said Grant's father. "The incumbent sheriff died of a heart attack while campaigning. If we vote for him they'll have to call a new election, with new opponents."

"Both live," smirked the woman of the pearls.

"Enough," her friend whispered to her. Grant thought he wasn't the only one who heard.

"I'll have the lemon pudding. How about you?" Grant's mother looked at him.

"Whatever you're having." Grant put his hand on hers. Her hair looked frizzy compared with the smooth silver upsweeps of the other ladies.

"The other guy is a nut." Eugene turned to the table of four women to his right.

"Which guy?" asked one of the women politely. She wore a yellow blouse buttoned high.

"The one running against the dead sheriff. He acts like the job is all a game, with his horse and ten-gallon hat."

"I don't think I understand," said the woman.

Grant realized that his father was asking people to vote against his own kind of nuttiness. Sadness overcame him. "What does a modern sheriff do?" he asked gently to divert his father.

"Dead or alive?" said Eugene, undiverted. Grant knew he had heard the whispering between the heckler and her friend. There was a sheen on his father's upper lip; his tie seemed bent; he clutched and unclutched his wide fingers.

"Dead," said Grant.

His father actually winked at the women. They tried to start a conversation of their own at their table.

Suddenly Eugene quit smiling. He leaned forward.

This is the moment, thought Grant. Each semester he drew a graph for his film students showing where the peak scenes should be placed.

"Old age should burn and rave at close of day," said his father, spoiling the line by nodding his head with the rhythm of it. "Isn't that what you were telling me the other day?"

"This isn't what I had in mind." Grant closed his eyes. When he was young, he had closed his eyes to make his father disappear. It had worked better then.

"I don't think Dylan Thomas has much to say to me," said Grant's mother. "He died at thirty-eight." Grant opened his eyes. Round spots of color had appeared on her cheeks.

Eugene hunched in a posture of betrayal. "What do you recommend?" he asked his wife.

"I think you two have to leave this place." Grant put both hands on the table. He lowered his voice. "It'll kill you. These aren't your kind of people. It's too confining."

"What are our kind of people?" asked Grant's mother. Her voice had the tinny edge that meant she was about to cry.

Grant couldn't speak. The couples at the next table scraped their chairs back and departed. The entire dining room was clearing out. The waiters, college kids who couldn't find better jobs, lounged along the wall, impatiently waiting for the last dishes.

"I've been thinking," said Grant's father. The sheen now covered his face. His napkin had fallen to the floor. "Do you know what's buried in Grant's heart?"

"Don't do this." Grant took a breath.

"Grant," said his father with exaggerated earnestness.

"Are you going to keep this up right to the end?" asked Grant.

"I'm going to keep on keeping on," said his father. He'd picked up certain sixties expressions and hadn't dropped them. They'd gotten a good play from the young people at his tennis club.

"I'm not selling the tools." Grant changed the subject, backing off. "I've decided I'll take them myself."

"My tools?"

"I want to keep them in case you need something fixed in the condo." There had to be something he could repair.

Eugene looked at his wife, then back at Grant. "They fix everything for us. That's in our plan." He was genuinely apologetic.

"Maybe I could fix it before they got to it. We can beat the plan." Grant smiled with effort.

"That would show them, wouldn't it?" Eugene said. For once, he looked right at his son and his face was uncontrolled. That moment, Grant thought that his father might cry but then a student reached between them and roughly took both plates. The moment was over.

Grant drove home with the exams on the floor of his Volvo, the toolbox bouncing heavily on the passenger's seat. He knew he had things backward but he left them as they were. His parents had stood in the circular driveway of The Cascades and hugged him too long. He felt trapped and exposed as other residents walked by.

The call came at eight the next morning. It was Grant's mother. At least she survived, thought Grant. He held his breath.

"The dead sheriff won," she said.

Grant asked her to repeat herself. His ears rang with the shock of the news that hadn't come.

She explained that now the election would be held again.

"How's Dad?" asked Grant. A former student stirred at his side. He patted her hip. He imagined that he was on both sides of a split screen: in one, he was tall and dark and his book-lined apartment gave off a rich, Bo Widerberg glow as a languid woman put her cheek on his knee and sighed; in the other, he was large and awkward in a low-rent studio with dirty windows and he spoke in a whisper so that a girl almost young enough to be his daughter wouldn't hear the quiver in his voice.

"The same as ever," his mother said.

"Has he made any friends at that place?"

There was a pause. "One. He's a banker too." She always said that her husband was part of the banking community, though he rarely went near his brothers' bank. Grant realized she had been looking for a community to claim for a long time.

The girl got up and went into the small bathroom. She had been a rotten student, no flair, no sense of possibility. But her papers were neat and grammatical and Grant had passed her.

"They're playing in the Bs at our first tennis tournament here."

"Who?" said Grant into the phone.

"Your father and his new friend. Grant, are you all right?"

"Not exactly. It's the beginning of the quarter. The students seem worse every term."

His mother was silent. Whenever he didn't speak the truth, she acted as if he hadn't spoken at all. "They're painting the living room today," she said brightly. "I picked Morning Green. It sounds nice and dewy."

"So you're staying," said Grant. "And that's all right with you."

Her silence had a different quality now. He could feel his mother gathering force. "You know, you think we're fools," she said tightly, "but you're the biggest fool of all."

Grant started to answer, then instantly forgot his response. His mother had rarely spoken harshly to him before. She never seemed to have strong opinions.

The girl leaned against the bathroom doorway in his shirt. She would crawl back into bed if he gave her the least chance. He nodded toward the kitchen and made a gesture of drinking coffee.

"I'm sorry," said Grant finally. "I guess I always expected you to leave him. Or something. I didn't think it would just all fade out."

"We've lived our lives," said his mother. "A lot has happened. You're the one who isn't living."

Her boldness must have come from sensing the end, Grant thought later. "I'm just exhausted," he said. "I'm always tired at the beginning of a new quarter."

His mother said nothing. Then she lapsed back into the mode they usually used with each other, of delivering the truth on a different plane. "I think students are more conservative these days, don't you? When I was a student, everything I learned seemed challenging, exciting. There was so much to do, so many places to go," she said. "Kids these days seem to worry more about stability. Maybe it's better."

"This is not a good time," Grant answered. "There's a department meeting in a half hour. I'll write."

"Sure," she said good-naturedly. "I'll believe it when I see it."

It wasn't his father who died but his mother. She had a stroke and lived for five days unable to talk. She blinked as a signal. Grant asked her if he could do anything for her. She blinked no. His father came to the bed and gave her a sip of water. She bent her head obediently for him. His parents had always been a team, Grant realized, and he felt doubly bereft.

Her clothes were in the bottom three drawers of the bureau. Her panties seemed so large and white compared with the colorful bikini briefs his girlfriends wore. He put her dresses on top of everything else in the suitcase, the hangers still in them. He asked his father if he should take the perfumes or if they could be given away. Eugene sat on the bed and didn't answer.

His father's banker friend had lost his wife fifteen years ago. His name was Luke. The three ate dinner together and no one else came near. Grant supposed that it was bad form to die in a place like this.

He stayed with Eugene for a week, reading a worn copy of *The Unknown Chekhov* that he found in the tiny library behind the dining room. He couldn't remember the last time he'd read a book for pure pleasure.

At home, he called his father every few days, then returned for a visit two months later. Eugene was a little better. He'd gotten a poker game going Friday nights and had skimmed off the better bridge players for the group.

Grant thought that grief had made his father shorter, more like Luke. They were sitting in the gallery seats of the indoor tennis court. Eugene wore a sweatband and a pair of shorts that minimized his belly. He and Luke had just won a place in the consolation-match finals. Luke sweated a lot and played slow, steady tennis. Eugene either hit the ball out or smashed a winner. They seemed to be favorites with the small but verbal crowd in the bleachers.

At first they sat in silence waiting for the next round. Then Luke said a glass of wine would make his bifocals work better. His delivery was good—he was the MC at most of the functions at The Cascades. He wandered off toward the refreshment table.

Eugene watched Luke go and wiped his face with a towel. "I'm sure glad we don't have a house to take care of," he said, turning to his son.

Grant understood that his father was asking for a concession. He took the towel and wiped his own hands. His family had not been one to backtrack like that. What was said was said. He found himself nodding yes. He braced himself against the little twist his father would give it but Eugene said nothing at first.

Then he put his foot on the bleacher seat in front of him. Without looking at Grant he said, "Your mother was scared one of us would start dying and I wouldn't know what to do. She thought I'd play the fool. She wanted other people around."

"She told you that?" Grant was amazed at his father's directness. He smelled his father's sweat, a deep but healthy smell.

"No, she didn't. We were married forty years. I knew."

Grant felt the largeness of the gymnasium, the echoing sounds. A strange giddiness grew in his head. Was his father trying to teach him something? Grant asked, "It was hard for you to move?"

Eugene nodded, his expression unchanged. "I didn't want you to know, because you would have told her."

So. Grant had missed the scene behind the scene. He
kissed his father's slack cheek, then awkwardly hugged him.
"You're a decent actor," he said softly.

The two men moved slightly away from each other and
Grant saw the profile that would be his own someday.

"A decent actor," Eugene said, patting Grant's shoulder.
The touch of his father's hand, the soft fingers, the surprisingly broad palm, brought a fine ache into Grant's throat.

He watched his father play tennis. Eugene wore socks that
came halfway to his knees and he grunted with glee when he
thought he had a clear shot. Three times he missed the ball altogether. He and Luke traded glasses. The little crowd laughed.

Grant hoisted his bag onto the bed and opened it. He put his
shirts away, folded his slacks, hung them up, and stowed the
suitcase in the cupboard where it belonged. Usually it took
him a week to straighten things out from a trip.

The toolbox lay open on the couch. He would completely
dismantle the haphazard boards and bricks of his bookcase to
make a wall unit. It would include a pull-out shelf for the TV
and a cupboard for the VCR and videotapes. He would need
the saw and drill, screwdrivers for the brackets, and the
heavy tape measure. He began to sketch the unit on a yellow
pad. Rich sunlight found the one high window in his apartment not blocked by other buildings. Finally Grant perfected
a design for a unit constructed in three parts; it would be
solid yet movable—he could take it with him when he finally
bought a house of his own. With a sigh Grant sat back on his
knees to admire his work. When he had started, he had
thought it couldn't be done.

Immortal Buttons

*T*he sun had just sent its rays across California to my tall house in the Los Altos hills. Venus still hung next to a faint moon. I was at the kitchen window watching the breeze bump two apples together on the tree outside—the greener one fell to the pebbled patio below and there was a rap at the screen door. As I turned to answer it I imagined the clutter of bottles, mismatched cups, dish towels, and coupons transformed into a neat row of mason jars filled with my own spicy applesauce.

It was my son, Andrew. He had filed for a divorce from his wife, Louise, the month before. He had told her that he needed to sort out his karma but I knew he just wanted to see his girlfriend openly. As he walked past me he said he needed a place to stay while Louise and he worked out the best terms for the dissolution.

An attorney, he was handling his own case. Soon after he walked out on Louise, he convinced her to move to a pink stucco apartment in Redwood City so he could sell their house. He claimed that having the cash would be best for her and Lisa and Freddy, their children.

I followed him up the stairs to the large, sunny bedroom that overlooks the apple trees and the patio. I hadn't slept in that room for thirty years, not since Andrew's father died.

In silence, Andrew set his elegant, soft luggage bag on the one clear space between my boxes of treasures. Like Louise, I become quiet around him. At any given moment he might turn the world into a courtroom, with prosecution on one side and defense on the other. He's the prosecutor; I'm the little old lady trembling on the stand who can be made to repeat whichever incriminating statement he chooses. So I try never to say anything too precise or definite around him, which is easy for me because there are few things that I feel certain about. I wasn't even absolutely sure that I didn't want him to move in.

The next day, Saturday, Andrew did a hundred sit-ups and jogged five miles through the foothills behind my house. I watched him as he drank a tumbler of unfiltered carrot juice. He's tall and has a bald spot, which was rimmed with sweat.

Still in his shorts and polo shirt, he cleaned out the dry rock pool at the far corner of the patio. He took the two mildewed canvas chairs and the old bicycle with the twisted handlebars to Goodwill. The Steller's jay that swoops from one apple tree to another squawked at all the commotion.

In my garage Andrew found the rusted pump for the waterfall that's supposed to fill the pool. He took it to the swimming supplies place to be repaired. He washed the crumbly moss off the decorative boulders and artfully rearranged them to look as if they had just tumbled down the grass slope at the edge of my property. He said, wouldn't it be nice when he got the waterfall running again.

I stood in the sun and nodded and shaded my eyes as I watched him. It seemed like it should be nice, but I thought of the evenings when I'd sit on the mossy rock and imagine the water slipping from boulder to boulder. In my mind I'd sing a tune that had no beginning and no end. It would be a sloshing, sparkling, dancing song that would glide from thunder to spray with no direction from me. I didn't think I could sing to tank water piped up the hill through a thick black hose.

My son found me in the study, where I had gone to think things over. He said he would help me clean out that room, too, although I hadn't been aware that I was going to clean it out. He hoisted onto his shoulder a large, dusty cardboard box of sheet music and grabbed a brown paper bag with the other hand.

"Wait," I said. If he was going to stay, certainly I needed to say something.

He turned.

"You can't just throw that away. First I need to sort out the articles with potential."

He smoothed back his hair, dark brown and coarse like mine before the gray. "What articles?" he said with a sigh.

I pulled at the edge of the bag and peered into it. A knot of rubber bands, cardboard beer coasters, two bundles of string. "These," I said, dragging out the string. "I'm going to dye and braid them and make treasure baskets to surprise Lisa and Freddy."

"When?" asked my son, gently prying the bag from my hands.

"When what?"

"When are you going to make the baskets? I've been hearing about that project for years." He straightened and went out to his red car, which was backed up to the entrance with its trunk open.

I shrugged as he heaved the box into the car. "Well, I can never make them now," I said.

He laughed as he slammed the door.

All that day and Sunday, too, he moved from room to room hauling out cartons of the mail-order catalogs I like to keep, clearing the drawers of makeup compacts and old Christmas cards and dragging stacks of mothballed clothes out of the closets. I ran after him trying to salvage what I could. I told him the pineapple corer really worked and just needed to be washed and put in its proper place in the kitchen. I was able to save only two Burpee seed packets with their glossy pictures of red, blue, and yellow blooms. He told me irritably that you couldn't count on the fertility of such old seeds anyway. Then he went upstairs and started on my former bedroom.

I put my hands to my mouth. I pictured the day my son would inherit this house, the ghosts of my belongings stacked all around him. I imagined standing before St. Peter with one small tote, as if I planned just to spend the night.

Panting a little, I began to climb the stairs. My husband had died of a stroke ten years after Andrew was born. Maybe that was when Andrew lost his sweet streak and the meanness set in. Or maybe I had just never noticed my son's rudeness until I went into mourning—until we went into mourning.

Up in the bedroom, Andrew was on his hands and knees swearing and picking up the buttons I'd saved from important pieces of clothing for the last thirty years. There, nestled in the green rug, one of the real deer-horn buttons that had been on my husband's hunting jacket. Lying next to the leg of the nightstand, the mother-of-pearl that had closed Louise's wedding gown at the back of her neck. Scattered by the door, the brass buttons of Andrew's first blazer, the one he wore when he graduated from La Entrada Elementary School.

I scooped up as many as I could and put them in the pockets of my dress. Andrew sat back on his haunches and gave me a stern look. I told him that these were immortal buttons.

His cheeks were red and sweat trickled down his forehead. In the last couple of years, his face had thickened. Although he didn't ask, I explained that buttons had more potential than most people knew. Even when the seat of the trousers wore out or the elbows of the jacket finally gave way, the buttons could be cut off and sewn onto something else. That way each new piece of clothing carried the dignity and character of the last. "You see?" I said, pocketing more of the buttons as Andrew tried to think of a diplomatic maneuver around his addled mother.

"I don't see these things having any new life," he said with not so much as a smile.

The smooth buttons felt like pebbles in my pockets. I let them run through my fingers. I'd just never managed to get the right button together with the matching color of thread and new item of clothing. Slowly, in clipped tones, my son told me that results were much more important than potential. He hoped I would understand that someday.

He left me kneeling on the floor as he took another load to Goodwill. I rested my back against the wall and pulled some of the buttons from my pocket to examine them. When had the chip appeared in the deer-horn wedge? How had the yellow plastic become cracked and the leather knots discolored? The last patch of sun receded from the floor and then was gone.

Andrew filled my refrigerator with domes of yogurt, which he ate instead of the good dinners I fixed. He said he needed to lose some of his gut. One morning after he'd gone to work I peeked into the bedroom just to see what he'd been doing up there. He had steamed off the wallpaper of pale climbing vines that framed my marriage bed and had painted the walls stark white. His gray computer screen was resting on the window seat. Several blue boxes burst on the screen and then disappeared. I ran my fingers across the keys while symbols danced before my eyes, finally stopping. A message flashed "Fatal disc error," and I jumped as a heavily accented voice intoned, "Hasta la vista, baby." I fled downstairs.

That evening as Andrew and I sat in the back room, he told me not to worry, there wasn't anything important on the computer anyway. "Why does it talk like that?" I tried to keep my voice from fading. He laughed as he used a sharp steak knife to remove the curling skin from an apple. He laid the peel on a red cocktail napkin he had found in one of my cupboards (had I been planning a party?). He took a bite, adjusted the blinders of the miniature television balanced on his knees, and stared at the picture. Still watching, he spooned a heavy mound of yogurt into his mouth, then withdrew the spoon with a smaller mound still on it. He did this several times until the spoon was clean. He took another bite of the apple.

"You shouldn't be afraid," I said. "I won't die in your arms." I planned to die dreaming in bed—no moaning, no mess. All he would have to do was peek in on me the morning he heard no sounds, tuck the cover under my chin, and call the coroner.

He looked up and laid the spoon across the yogurt dome. "Mother," he said. "What are you talking about?" He hadn't called me Mother since he'd moved in. I was reminded of a shy child who had told me through tears that he didn't need to go to school, because I could teach him everything.

"May I have your peel?" is all I said. "It's the sweetest, most nutritious part."

He held out the napkin, then turned off the television. There was a faint click and the light from the screen left his face. He leaned toward me. "Why have you let yourself go like this?"

Let myself go? My hand wandered to my face, my hair. My eyes traveled to the spot on the lampshade that looked like a single wing. I thought of the caked face powder, the orphan buttons, the unopened sheet music, the rotten apples smeared on the patio. I turned away from my son.

He left his place and knelt beside my chair, fumbling in his shirt pocket. He tucked a plastic card into my fingers. Startled, I held up the little maroon plaque so I could read it. There was my name in raised letters. My son had gotten me a charge card.

"Buy yourself some clothes," he said.

Did I need clothes?

Andrew saw my expression and his smile vanished. "When I was younger," he said, "I always thought I would buy you a house." Now he looked about to cry.

"You don't like this house?"

He patted his forehead with the back of his hand. "I thought we would have a maid to do the cleaning and bathe the children. My wife would go shopping with you."

Louise hates to shop, as I do.

He bent his head. I felt his profound disappointment in me, yet for the first time, I realized he was glad to be home.

"Tomorrow I'll get the waterfall running." He spoke softly, watching my face. "And Jocelyn will come over and cook. Won't that be festive?"

"Festive" was a word I used. He got up and crumpled the red napkin. I didn't want his girlfriend in my kitchen throwing out the old spices, but I nodded to my balding, paunchy son. I slid the card into a pocket and told him yes, it would be fun to have company for a change.

It wasn't at all. Watching Jocelyn cook made me dizzy. Chop, chop, chop, wipe hands on the towel, sprinkle soy sauce in the wok (she'd brought her own pans), stir, turn, set out tableware, taste the simmering vegetables, answer Andrew's call from the backyard for another glass of chardonnay, stir again, sip iced water, and smile at me.

I smiled back. She was a temporary paralegal in Andrew's office, and I pictured her efficiently pulling documents from his files. She had assigned me the task of hors d'oeuvres while she cooked and Paul worked on the waterfall. When it became clear that I wasn't going to finish before dinner, she told me graciously that my offerings would be just as good with the meal, as side dishes.

As I struggled with the pineapple corer, she helped me plunge it into the prickly skin and extract a perfect cylinder of woody fruit. I spread a layer of pineapple chunks on the plate she handed me and put a toothpick in each cube. Finished with that, I shoved the plate aside and bent four toothpicks in half and placed them flat on the table so that the broken joints of the toothpicks touched while the sharp tips pointed outward.

"Oh, a star." Jocelyn glanced at the toothpicks and whisked away the plate of fruit. She had blond hair that flipped back from her face, and she told me, as she popped a pineapple piece in her mouth, that she'd been accepted at law school.

I began to make another star on the Formica kitchen table. That morning I'd found an eyedropper in the bathroom cabinet. A little water at the center of the star would make the wood swell. I remembered a small boy who wanted a star every morning next to his cornflakes.

"How old are you?" I asked her.

Jocelyn frowned at me and didn't answer. She yelled at Andrew that he'd better get the thing going pretty soon or we'd have to eat before the christening. Without waiting, she scooped the steaming vegetables into a pale yellow dish she'd found under the sink. I sipped my wine and went to work on the radishes Jocelyn handed me. I liked the smell of her floral perfume and told her so. She smiled again and said it was Giorgio to show I was forgiven for my question about her age.

We worked in silence for some time. I presented her with a dozen perfect radish roses and then she asked me to go out back and get Andrew—dinner couldn't wait any longer.

Picking up a radish for the jay, I opened the French doors. Andrew stood with one foot on the boulder that edged the waterfall on the right, the other foot on the stone apron of the small pool. A rotten apple was next to his heel. He wore Top-Siders. Suddenly water gurgled down the concrete chute. "Eureka," he said. His face shone with sweat and a joy I had not seen in years.

He bent over and adjusted the thick electrical cord for the pump so that it was better concealed behind the boulder. Startled by the sound of water, the jay fluttered out of the apple tree and made a pass at Andrew. He teetered, then regained his footing.

I set the radish down on the patio and the jay soared over and plucked it from the pebbled surface while I told Andrew to come to dinner.

"Don't feed that bird, Mother." He looked around. "They carry lice." He stepped toward me off the boulder, slipped on the apple, and went straight down as if one thin thread had held him up all this time. Without a word, he struck his head against the boulder and landed with his face under the cascade of water.

The liquid sluiced against his eyes and into his nose and open mouth. He breathed it in and gagged but remained unconscious. I ran to him, braced myself against the rock, placed my hand beneath his neck, and pulled him away from the waterfall. The collar of his sopping shirt flopped open. Water spilled out of the shell of his ear. I was the only one who could save him.

Coughing, he opened his eyes and gasped cool air. I was soaked as if I, too, had almost drowned. As Andrew raised his arms for me to help him stand, I saw an eager boy sitting in his pajamas at the kitchen table. The toothpick stars I had made the night before were laid out for him. There were dozens of them. A drop of water quivered at the end of the eyedropper I held. "Do it!" he said.

With my wand, I circled the table and touched each center. All over the Formica the stars swelled and the constellation grew, and Andrew stood up on the chair and hugged himself, and then me.

Breathe at
Every Other Stroke

*B*efore he met Helen, Stewart never knew what to do with Saturday afternoons. His subcontractors went home by three. He would climb onto the roof and make sure the tarps over the skylight cuts would hold through Sunday, then drive to his apartment on Seattle's Capitol Hill for a long shower. He might walk down to Lake Washington, a Heineken in one hand, and watch the hydroplanes. Secretly, he always thrilled at the thought of one's flipping over, tossing the flimsy driver onto water that became concrete with the force of the body's fall. But he never saw an accident, and hours later he would wander home through streets that seemed longer in the darkness.

As he walked, Stewart sometimes imagined that his father's face had appeared in the water. In the daydream, Stewart was underwater too. The bleary eyes swam up to him and he could smell the gin and hear the snuffling sound of the man's breathing.

Stewart's father was a careless man. Once he drove a car over the end of the Deception Pass bridge, but the wheels caught in a bush and he survived. He forgot to go to work for days at a time. When drunk enough, he would swim naked at night in the icy water of Lake Washington, and Stewart would find him later dripping and shivering in the living room, an oddly exultant look on his face.

One morning when Stewart was eighteen his father didn't come home at all. His mother sat motionless at the kitchen table absently holding the headset of Stewart's Walkman near her cheek. A tiny voice giving the traffic report emanated from the earphones, making the kitchen seem close, eerie. Stewart busied himself putting away the soggy groceries his mother had bought the day before. "They haven't found him yet," she said. "I wonder if he finally drowned." Stewart thought she was trying out the words to see if she could bear them. He peeled the plastic bag from the ice-cream carton and ran water through the slush. She turned off the radio. "I've got you," she said. "That's something he never really had." Stewart thought then that someday he'd move to the mountains, but a decade passed and he had stayed in Seattle.

He met Helen through work, stopping at her house to deliver a quote for installing a window greenhouse in the south wall of her kitchen. The messiness of her place seemed rich compared with the stark functionalism of his. They got to talking about the hydroplane races on Seafair Days and she asked if he would take her to see them.

She brought along a bowl of potato salad and they ate large mounds of it as the deafening roar of boats sucked their conversation out into the lake. She had broad shoulders, from her swimming days at Tacoma High, she said, and hated her job as a secretary because she was a people person, not a file person. Although he rarely talked about his father, Stewart blurted out a memory of walking the edge of the dark lake all night calling for him. Helen's eyes watered and she said that her father visited every other Saturday when he was in town.

Stewart dabbed at her tears with a paper napkin. He watched her curved upper lip as she sucked a potato chunk from her fingers. Feeling giddy, he dipped his thumb in the Tupperware bowl and licked the mayonnaise from his knuckle.

At the end of the greenhouse job, Helen moved a deep couch into the new crisscrossed rectangle of pale Seattle light. Laughing, she said it would make the kitchen a multipurpose room and invited Stewart over for a conjugal lunch, as she called it. Stewart was supposed to meet a client about some expensive gallery windows. For the first time, he asked the foreman to call and say he had the flu.

Helen greeted him at the door wearing only shoes and a long gauzy shirt. It was the kind of thing his father would have done, but God in heaven, Helen didn't look anything like his father. Stewart glimpsed her bare skin under the cloth as she moved. He lowered his eyes. Her feet arched down into bright satin slippers with bands across the toes. Each band held a red puff ball that seemed to float. She said she'd gotten them at Woolworth's as a joke. Stewart felt overwhelmed with tenderness toward the cheap slippers. Trying hard not to tremble, he sat on the couch. Helen disappeared and he thought he was going to cry, but she quickly came back and handed him a bologna sandwich. He asked if she'd ever been married and instantly wished he hadn't been so nervous, pushy, but she suddenly looked serious and said, "Not yet."

Happy, he lifted her foot and blew on one of the puffs. "These look like bedroom shoes," he said.

She touched his chin and laughed. "No, multipurpose."

Within weeks, Helen was pregnant. The night after the wedding, Stewart impulsively asked if she wanted to move to the mountains. He'd been thinking that ski bums in Sun Valley could provide cheap labor for his business. She loved the idea of moving. She could become a ski instructor. He imagined his sign, Skycatcher Enterprises, set on the front lawn of their mountain home and pictured the bright patches of sunlit space he'd turn into luxurious vacation houses.

Three months later they moved, and Stewart felt like a new man—he'd finally gotten to the mountains. But Helen's belly got larger and larger and she didn't decorate their cabin in the tiny town of Ketchum, the poor cousin of the ski resort, the only neighborhood they could afford. She barely unpacked. He hadn't realized that she'd bring her disheveled ways to the mountains. Then the baby came, an impatient bundle of greed.

It was 4:00 A.M. and Stewart's turn to feed him. The snow had drifted down over Mount Baldy for two days and three nights. A stiff breeze blew against the mountain, scooped up the top layer of crystals, and tossed them on the roof. Stewart fed baby Paul and watched the snowstorm swirl against the skylight bubble overhead. He'd put the window in himself. It didn't leak. His work was perfect.

Stewart sat on the sofa from Seattle. Helen's damp ski clothes were piled on the floor. Magazines, Chinese-food containers, and half-empty boxes crowded the room. Stewart imagined the weight of the water pressing in on his father from all sides. He thought of the involuntary heaving of the chest and the final snap of the will, the first great gulp of water.

The skiers he'd hired so far had made terrible carpenters. On a sunny day they would drop their tools and head for the slopes. And most of the vacation homes belonged to absentee owners who paid late from distant banks. Then there was the complication of the baby.

The memory of the birth burned fresh, as if it had just happened or was about to begin at any moment. He could still smell the blood and the starch of the gown a nurse had pulled on him and see the red vessels in Helen's eyes as she pushed. She held his wrists but he felt useless next to her powerful heaving body. Then she shouted, "Paul, come out!" and there was the bloody head, the swimming arms, and Stewart knew that his wife and son were blind swimmers groping for him, for his steadiness.

The baby squirmed in his father's hands and threw himself to the side so that the bottle rammed into his ear. He screamed. Stewart tried to hold the small writhing body close to his chest but Paul pushed out with his sticky hands. Stewart carried him to the kitchen sink and gave him his first bath in two days. Helen contended that infants didn't get very dirty. All day she sang and talked nonsense and skied cross-country with Paul in a pouch at her chest. She said he was a happy baby. It hadn't occurred to Stewart that someone so small could be happy or not.

In the dryer Stewart found a terry sleeper and pulled it on over the baby's head. He snapped the leggings of the pajamas closed, moving the child carefully. Helen appeared in the hallway. She wore one of Stewart's shirts over her nightgown with a kimono over that. She looked like a woman built up in layers. "Any trouble?" she asked, leaning against the wall. She was barely awake. Unlike Stewart, she slept well when it wasn't her turn to feed the baby.

Stewart couldn't describe the trouble. Helen's large hands hung loosely at her sides. She was one of the few people capable of standing and doing nothing. "Why are you mad at me?" she asked, folding her arms. She stepped into the Woolworth's slippers. Their red was dulled, the puffs matted.

"I'm not mad at you." Stewart put the child lengthwise along his thighs. Paul had fallen into his uneasy early-morning sleep. With his eyes closed, he snuffled, sighed, and panted.

Helen sat beside him. The baby woke with a start. She picked him up and squinched her features into a baby monster face. The infant waved his arms at her, as if greeting a fellow being. Stewart felt like the alien. He just had to keep things going so these two could play.

"You want me to do something and I don't know what it is," Helen said. "It's not fair." She'd used a fake pout to tease him out of arguments before, but it had become a habit.

"I want you to get rid of those shoes now that we have the baby. You'll fall."

She nuzzled the baby, repeating his grunts and groans in a high, unearthly voice. Baby Paul watched her closely. He never seemed to focus on Stewart. "I won't fall," she said. She bent and, with one hand, threw a log in the almost dead fire. "Why did you let it get so cold in here?" Standing up, she strutted a little in the slippers.

Without the baby Stewart felt empty. "Get out of those damn shoes," he said. He imagined the snow getting so heavy it slid down the mountain and the three of them were swimming in the avalanche, trying to keep up with the speed of the snow.

"You're not much fun anymore," she said. The words were from her pouting days but they were dry. Although the veins had healed, Helen's eyes were still puffy.

With the baby on one arm, she began to walk back over to Stewart, then, seeing that he wasn't going to answer, wheeled dramatically, fanning the fight. She started to say something, but before the end of the sentence she tripped on a box of books. As the child went down, she snatched at his leg and saved him from hitting the floor, but the bone snapped with the sound of a breaking twig. Helen screamed. She clutched the shrieking baby with both arms and kicked at the shoes, sending one spurting up toward the skylight, its old puff quivering in flight. "What have I done?" she wailed after the shoe.

Hurriedly, Stewart wrapped the terrified baby in a blanket, holding his leg at the diaper-padded hip so that the bent limb was still. Helen, crying, drove the mile to the Sun Valley emergency clinic, the wheel grasped tightly in both hands. The baby's screams made the road seem, somehow, icier to Stewart. He winced again at the smallness of the snapping sound as the leg had broken. It was nothing, but it exploded in Stewart's mind, warning of danger in every nook, reaching for him. Anything could happen. His vigilance was only a fine, irrelevant membrane between his son and the sudden flip into blackness.

The doctors and nurses, who usually treated ski injuries, asked a lot of questions. Helen was stricken. Stewart sat beside her in the waiting room, feeling his sweat slide down into the plastic chair. Vigilance, he thought. Vigilance.

Later, the baby slept between them at home on their couch, his leg stiff against the cushion. The clumsiness of the cast emphasized the perfection of his limbs. His pale pink cheek rested on old bread crumbs. Stewart thought of Seattle, lifted the boy gently, and brushed away the crumbs. Paul's light breath touched his wrist. Think, he commanded himself, but his mind wandered numbly.

Helen wore her ski jacket over the kimono. Her remorse made her silent and unbending. She looked stiffly to one side; Stewart gazed away to the other. The baby seemed to repel them at the center.

"What happens now?" she said finally.

Stewart couldn't concentrate on the question. Paul snuffled at his side. The body of Stewart's father wasn't found for a week, as if even in death, he were able to hide out longer than most. There was nothing Stewart could have done to keep his father at home. This thought was so startling that it crowded out the moment with Helen and the baby.

Picking up a sweater, Helen smoothed it over the back of the chair to dry. She collected the other clothes around the room, folded them, and placed them on the seat. "The world could end tomorrow," she said and came back to the couch.

It was dawn, but snow covered the glass above, making the room shadowy. Stewart looked at her and nodded. Then he nodded again.

This seemed to surprise her and give her strength. "The world really could end tomorrow." She lifted her hair from her neck.

Paul waved an arm, turned his head. His eyes moved under bluish lids.

"I know," Stewart said. He had thought that his job was to stave off fate. Now he saw a different use for the unknown future. "Don't we have to act as if it won't end?" He felt the same giddiness as when he first met Helen.

She turned toward him.

Feeling the beginnings of a silly smile, Stewart watched the baby's slowly rotating arms. Helen followed his gaze. Finally Stewart said, "What do you think he dreams about?"

She looked up at him quickly. Her features relaxed. "I think he dreams about an indoor pool."

They hadn't focused on each other since Paul was born, Stewart realized. He thought of the two winter swimming pools in Sun Valley. They were outdoors but heated.

Snowflakes fell on the steaming heads of the bathers. "Will you teach me how to swim?" he asked.

A teasing look came over Helen's face. The baby would look like her. "You don't know how to swim?"

"Not even float."

"I'm married to a man who can't swim." Gently she patted baby Paul's small stomach and laughed.

"Not yet," said Stewart, eyeing her.

She looked at him, leaned over the sleeping baby, and whispered, "How would you like to see Daddy in a Speedo?"

I'd like to thank MaryLee McNeal for her wisdom and friendship, and Deborah Thomson for the postcard that always says yes. My deepest thanks also to Lettie Lee and Sara Bershtel, and to Riva Hocherman.